# A Crazy Ghetto Love Story 2
## The Killing Spree

## Written By:
## Linette King

D1444478

A Crazy Ghetto Love Story 2
The Killing Spree
-A Novel Written By-
Linette King
Copyright © 2016 by True Glory Publications
Published by True Glory Publications
Join our Mailing list by texting TrueGlory to 95577

Facebook: Author Linette King

Cover Design: Dottie D'Zigns
Editor: Artessa La'Shan Michelé

## Acknowledgements

Major shoutout and big thanks to God who is the head of my household. To God be the glory. With God with me who can be against me?

To my children: Aaliyah, Alannah and Jaye! When I first had you guys I didn't for one second think I would be doing the single mom thing. As you grow and experience life you will understand why I've always worked so hard. I know I work a lot but I have to make sure you guys have everything you need and want! Time flies and I just want you to take your time and live life according to your happiness. Never ever lean on someone else for happiness. It has to come from within. I want you guys to know that I will always have your back no matter what. It doesn't matter what anyone says I want you to remember 2 things: Keep God first and mommy loves you!!!

To my family: Pooh, Mama, Oliver, and Ms. Peggy, you guys have been so supportive but it didn't just start now. Yall have always been there for me and my kids going above and beyond to help make sure those smiles stayed on their faces. I love you!

To my friends: Jasmine, Trinisha, and Ashleigh, I have no earthly idea how yall put up with me on a daily basis but I'm glad yall do. Yall are each extremely crazy so it balances me out.

To Shameek: I thank you so much for opening this door for me to be able to do something I love! I enjoy working with you and you have become like a big brother to me. It still amazes me how someone you just met can have better intentions for you than people you've known your whole life.

To my readers: Thanks for reading and I hope you enjoy this series! Don't forget to leave a review please! If you haven't read Addicted to him yet, stop what you're doing and download it right now! It's a great read if I may say so myself. Find me @

goodreads.com Linette King where I will be answering questions daily. Find me on facebook @ facebook.com/?_rdr#!/2tsworld/?ref=bookmarks and like my author page. Send my regular facebook a friend request which is also Linette King here's the link facebook.com/linette.king.35 and feel free to hit me up with any questions, concerns or comments about my books. Thanks again!

This story is completely a work of fiction. Anything that resembles any real life event or person is purely coincidental. Enjoy!

# A CRAZY GHETTO LOVE STORY 2
## THE KILLING SPREE

## Steve

I was so happy Michael didn't kill me after he caught me snooping around his room and even happier that he trusted me enough to help him find his daughter. Imagine my surprise when we pulled up to this building that was abandoned. "What are we doing here?" I asked, as I took in my surroundings. "Ouch!" I said, as I jumped and grabbed my arm. Michael had given me a shot of something and it burned. "What was that?" I asked. My mouth started to feel extremely dry, along with my eyeballs.

"C'mon, we have to hurry," Michael said, as he hopped out the car before jogging to my side of the car. He opened my door and pulled me out. My mind told me something wasn't right but my body wasn't comprehending that I needed to run. He led me through a spacious room, down a hallway, and through a door, half dragging me. It felt like my legs were going out but they kept moving. There was a long table centered in the room. Michael lifted my body before lying me on the table. I tried to get up but I could no longer move anything. "What's happening to me?" I asked.

"I gave you succinylcholine in shot form to paralyze you temporarily. Don't worry, it will wear off on its own," he explained, while he strapped me down.
"If I'm paralyzed, then why are you tying me down?" I asked, wishing I could go back in time and never moved in with him.

"It's better to be safe than sorry," he said winked after he had me restrained securely.

It seemed like we sat in that room together forever before he left out. While he was gone, I took the chance of trying to break free but I still couldn't move. When he returned to the room, I didn't want to look at him. I already saw the surgical tools on the small table and I didn't want him to use them on me. *Since I can't move, I know I won't be able to feel it,* I thought to myself.

"Steve?" I heard Phat ask. When I looked over and saw the very people I tried to have killed all standing before me, my eyes filled with fear. Frankie had tears streaming down her cheeks and if I could go back and right any wrongs, it would be involving her. Frankie wasn't the type of person that should have been doing any of the shit we've been doing all of our lives. She was better than that. She was better than us.

"So, I've found out a few things you guys probably want to know that Steve may or may not disclose," Michael said, as Phat and Chris stared at me like they wanted to kill me. I'm pretty sure they're going to.

"Why man?" Phat asked. It took me a second to realize he was talking to me. I looked between him and Chris, both stood there like their shit didn't stink! I refuse to answer any questions! *Fuck them!* I thought to myself as I looked away.

"I think jealousy, for some reason," Michael said, which caused my blood to boil. I'm not jealous of these bitches! I'm the reason they had somewhere to stay, so why would I be jealous? I'm the reason Chris and Phat had their own rooms! James and I slept from couch to couch and they always looked down on us! They shared all of their bitches with each other but never passed them to me or James. I'm not jealous. I'm pissed!

"You guys robbed a few houses over in Newark. Steve told them it was James and his crew. They caught up to James and told him to bring you guys to them. I don't know why you all didn't show up or what happened, but it was all a setup," Michael explained to them. My heart began to beat rapidly in my chest. *How the hell he find all that shit out?* I questioned myself. If it wasn't for Alexis stopping Phat from coming and that skinny bitch saving them, I wouldn't be in the situation I'm in now.

"Vanessa, the guy's brother they robbed is the guy that hired you to kill the guys that were about to kill them. He had no idea that you were going to show up the same night as the setup. He was trying to kill two birds with one stone. Allowing his brother to kill them and for you to kill his brother would have put him on top. After his plan backfired, he linked up with the lady that drives cab 4141. I've tried to get close enough to her to see her face but every time I try, she pulls off. I normally only see her watching one of you guys," Michael said, which caused my eyes to get big.

I began to put everything together in my head. I turned slightly to look at Vanessa and realized she had the same height and build as the girl that saved Chris and Frankie that night. Michael just said she was hired to kill the people that were going to kill Chris. *Michael has one fucked up family*, I thought to myself. No wonder everyone is crazy, hell, look at what Michael did to me. So, he has that son Wayne who may be the only normal one. Then there's Princess, who is missing, and Vanessa, who kills people, and is dating a nigga that robs people. Talk about your fixer upper.

"Any questions?" Michael asked.

"We need to find the guy that hired me that night, so we can figure out who this woman is," Vanessa said.

Shit, I want to know who this woman is too. "Ok, do what you want with him," Michael said, stepping on the other side of the table I was strapped to.

"You brought your bag Nessa?" Chris asked, and I knew shit was about to get real! I saw what this crazy bitch did to that lady we kidnapped and gave her for her birthday.

"Of course. It's in the truck. I'll run out and get it," Vanessa said happily as she walked away heading towards the door.

BOOM! The sound of something exploding scared me so bad; I closed my eyes real tight. It was involuntary, I guess, since I couldn't move anything else. When I opened my eyes, everyone was on the floor except the people dressed in all black that were filing into the room. I watched in horror as the room filled with smoke and two masked men headed in my direction. They pushed the table I was on towards the door and I could see someone kneeling over Vanessa. *Please kill that crazy bitch*, I thought to myself.

"You want me to kill her boss?" a deep male voice asked the person kneeling over Vanessa. *Please say yes boss*, I thought to myself.

"Not yet. It's too easy this way." I heard a female voice say.

"Mom?" Vanessa asked before she passed out.

*It's official. Their whole fucking family are nuts!* I thought to myself as the guys pushed me out the building and in the back of a van. I wanted to ask them where they were taking me but I didn't want to piss them off. If this crazy lady threw a bomb in the room with her daughter in it; I know she don't care about anyone at all. She probably doesn't care about life.

Wait! Michael told me she died and that's why they don't have any pictures of the family in their house! "What the fuck is going on?" I mumbled to myself.

We rode for hours in the back of the van with nobody saying anything to anyone. The part of the van I was in had no windows, so I had no idea where we were. All I know is we were bumping and bouncing all over the place back here.

We finally slowed down and I heard the window roll down. "Oh, I'm sorry boss, I didn't know it was you. Everything ok?" someone asked.

"Yes, I'm fine, thank you," the boss said before I heard the window again.

"Open up!" I heard someone yell before the van started moving again. When it finally came to a stop, the masked men stood up and hopped out the back of the van.

"Lock him up." I heard the boss say. The masked men returned to the back of the van and wheeled the table out.

I could hear the gravel underneath the table as they pushed it towards the biggest mansion I had ever seen in my life! It was so big; I couldn't see all of it. It looked like a tall iron gate surrounded the entire property with guards walking back and forth between their posts. On the other side of the gate was nothing but trees. *This is how you hide out!* I thought to myself as I continued to look around.

The doors to the mansion opened on their own as I rode through still laying on the table. The boss was living luxurious with high ceilings and a winding staircase. The masked men pushed me into an elevator and we went down to the ground floor. It looked like another house down here.

"This where you stay," one of the masked men asked with a weird accent.

"Where you from?" I asked, frowning.

Chuckling lightly, he said, "Slovakia," while unstrapping me. I tried moving off the table but still could not move anything but my head. "What they give you?" the man from Slovakia asked.

"Some shit to paralyze me temporarily," I answered.

"Boss not gone like this," the man said walking away. The other guy followed him without saying a word.

I instantly regretted opening my mouth because I didn't know what the boss would do to me because of this. I looked around and wished I could move my limbs, so I could explore. My stomach began to growl and I know I couldn't feed myself, and I didn't want a grown man feeding me either. Hell, I can't even let anyone know I'm hungry. Confusion and anger set in as I lay paralyzed on a table inside of the boss' mansion.

**Chris**

"Man, what the fuck just happened?" I snapped, sitting up. My damn head was killing me as I looked around the room. Phat was getting up as well but Frankie was already up and crying. She been doing that crying shit a lot lately. I looked towards the door and saw Vanessa's body stretched out. I hopped up and ran as fast as my legs would take me to her. She was still breathing but unconscious.

"Yo, she good?" Phat asked.

"Yea, what about her dad?" I asked, since Phat was checking on him.

"He good," he said, standing to his feet before helping her dad up.

"Let's get out of here," I said, scooping Vanessa up. We all headed out to the truck except Vanessa's dad, Michael. He hopped in the car that he drove here in. I buckled Vanessa up and hopped in the passenger's seat with Phat driving, and Frankie and Alexis in the back with Vanessa. When I looked back at them, Frankie was still crying silently. Alexis stared at the floor and Vanessa was still out of it. It took us about thirty minutes to get to our house and Michael pulled in behind us.

Everyone filed out of the truck without saying anything to each other as I grabbed Vanessa and carried her inside. "Is she good?" Michael asked, following me to her room.

"Yea, she just has to wake up," I said, tucking her in. When I turned around, Michael was smiling. "What?" I asked, confused.

"You love my daughter, don't you?" he asked, causing to me actually think about it.

"I care about her wellbeing," I said, walking passed him, heading into the living room. I was not about to have that kind of conversation with him when she and I aren't even on that kind of level.

She won't let the past go and unless she did, we couldn't be together and it's not even because I don't want to. The crazy thing was that I wanted to see where it could go with her. We live together and we do everything together that couples do, except fuck. She's still claiming she's a virgin and even got Alexis backing up her story, but ain't nobody our age a damn virgin. Everybody fucking or has before.

"What we gone do about this?" I asked, after we were all in the living room. Nobody answered me as I looked around the room. Everyone was in their own world like shit ain't just get real! "Do anybody know who it was or why they did it?" I asked, looking at everyone. Phat and Alexis shook their heads, Michael looked away and Frankie was still crying. "Man chill out with all that crying shit Frank! Them tears ain't gone change shit, man. The fuck you crying for?" I snapped, causing her jaw to drop. She cried harder, which pissed me completely off!

"It was my mom," Vanessa said, causing me to look at her crazy. They told me her mama was dead. Now, they expect me to believe her dead ass mama is alive, threw a grenade at us, and took Steve!

"Man that's bullshit! I went to the funeral with you!" Alexis said, jumping up with tears running down her face. Phat grabbed her but she snatched away from him. "There's no way that's your mama Vanessa; she's dead! She had an open casket funeral; I remember!" Alexis yelled.

"We probably imagined it was her Lexi; I was only eight," Vanessa said with tears welling up in her eyes. I looked over at Michael, who hadn't said a word or even looked up.

"No, you imagined it was her today!" Alexis said with finality. Maybe she's right though. If Vanessa's mother died when she was eight and they had an open casket, then more than likely, she imagined seeing her today. It could have all been a dream. Looking in Vanessa's eyes right now though; I did not want to be the one telling her that. Shit, Alexis shouldn't even be telling her that. The man sitting here as quiet as a church mouse supposed to be telling her that shit!

"Ya'll going back and forth like your daddy ain't sitting right here! Ask him!" I snapped, causing both of them to look at Michael. He sent me a look of death before returning their stare.

"Karen's dead baby girl," he said, shaking his head.

"See!" Alexis said. "I know you wish she wasn't but she is," Alexis said, walking up to Vanessa. She reached her arms out to hug her, but Vanessa pushed her and walked off. She pushed her hard too. If Phat wouldn't have caught her, I'm sure she'd be hurting pretty bad.

I watched as Vanessa stormed down the hall without looking back to see if she had hurt Alexis or not. Emotions were high right now and I was not about to go back there and talk to her. I know Vanessa and I know when she's upset, she gets violent, so I'm staying the fuck from round her. Alexis leaned in Phat's arms and began to cry, and Michael got up and left. Frankie shocked the fuck out of me when her little scary ass got up to go check on her. *I'm not staying around to watch this shit*, I thought to myself as I grabbed my car keys and headed out the door.

Some kind of way I ended up back at Brittany's house. All bullshit aside, Brittany was cool as fuck but she tried too hard to get a man. She thought if she put the pussy on you good enough, it would keep you coming back and in my case, it would. I liked this no strings attached shit with her because she didn't like me like that. I gave her the dick and she gave me the pussy, but everybody around here knows she's in love with Phat. Of course, Alexis or Vanessa ain't gone let that happen. I know Phat and I know as soon as he gets a chance, he will be fucking Brittany again. He just needs to tell her to get her feelings in check and stop that hoe shit, or Vanessa may kill her.

"Back so soon?" Brittany asked, taking a seat on the steps.

"Shit's hectic back home," I answered plainly. I didn't want to be bothered with that shit, especially if nobody else cared. Everybody's sitting around like a bitch ain't just throw a damn grenade in the room with us. Plus, I had to figure out how I'm going to make my money now that it's only Phat, Frankie, and I. I might as well count Phat out because Alexis got him under lock and key. Shit, I might as well count Frankie out too; the way she's been carrying on lately.

"What's going on?" Brittany asked, like she's really concerned. I sat between her legs on the steps and leaned my body against hers as I sighed heavily.

"Nothing," I said, not trusting anyone outside of the people I just left. It's moments like this with Brittany I can fuck with though. The only time I can't fuck with Brittany is when she step out of her lane. I don't have time for a bitch to be in her feelings. If she was feeling me like she's feeling Phat, I wouldn't even be here right now.

I closed my eyes as she began to scratch my head. "C'mon, let me take care of you," she whispered in my ear. I stood up and allowed her to lead me to an apartment and to the back room. She pushed me on the bed and pulled my jeans and boxers down around my ankles. I watched her take my semi hard dick in her mouth and suck it to life. Brittany was sucking my dick like her life depended on it, while humming the Christmas song *Jingle Bells*. The vibrations from her throat was killing me as she sucked up and down my shaft slowly without missing a beat. She lightly massaged my balls with her hand while sucking and humming. I squeezed my eyes closed tight while trying to focus on something else. Anything else! She started sucking harder and I released down her throat.

I laid across the bed panting and when I opened my eyes, Brittany was standing in front of me naked with a smile on her face. The left side of her face was still slightly swollen and bruised, but I'm not sure if Alexis did it or Vanessa. I'd put my last dollar on Vanessa though. Her small ass had a big lick!

"Are you ready for more?" she asked, as she looked down at me. My dick started rising, answering her question. She straddled me slowly before she positioned herself over my dick. I pushed her off of me and hopped up. "What the fuck Chris?!" she yelled, getting off the floor. I didn't try to push her on the floor, just off of me.

"Bitch, you know better!" I snapped, as I stuffed my dick in my pants. Bitch thought she was slick trying to sit on my dick with no protection! She got me fucked all the way up.

"Wait! What I do?" she yelled, running behind me as I headed out the door. "Chris wait! I'm sorry!" she pleaded. I glanced back at her standing naked on the steps and shook my head.

"I don't know what the fuck I was thinking coming here," I said out loud to myself.

## Brittany

I've been dealing with Chris for years, so I don't know why he does me this way. People think I'm a hoe but the truth is, I'm not. I'm just in love with two men that I can't have. It's really like, at this point, I'll take what I can get. I've been praying every night that I'm pregnant because then I'll be a part of Phat's life forever. That night we had sex and the condom broke made all my dreams come true!

*I was sitting outside on the steps with my girls Alisha and Stephanie. We don't have shit else to do when we ain't trying to snag a baller, so we hang outside together. "Why don't you ever want to hit the mall with us?" Stephanie asked me.*

*"Because you hoes ain't got no damn money!" I answered rolling my eyes.*

*"Bitch, you neither!" Alisha snapped, rolling her neck.*

*"Exactly! The fuck my broke ass gone do at the mall?" I asked, patiently waiting on an answer when my phone started ringing.*

*"Long time no hear," I said answering the phone, shocked that he was even able to break away from that bitch long enough to call me. It had been months since I've had some of Phat's dick and I was missing it like crazy! That stuck up ass girlfriend of his stayed glued to his hip, so I wasn't able to slide in.*

*"Where you at?" he asked.*

*"Around the corner from you. Want me to come through?" I asked with my fingers crossed. Alisha and Stephanie were both staring in my face trying to figure out who I was talking to.*

*"Naw, I'm out walking around trying to clear my head. I'll be over there in a few," he said, then hung the phone up.*

*"AAAAhhhh! Yes! Girl, my man fina come through! I've been missing him so much!" I screamed with joy. I can't begin to describe the feeling Phat gives me just by looking in his eyes! Those perfect grey eyes make me fall in love with him all over again.*

*"Bitch who?" Alisha asked, causing me to smile harder.*

*"Phat!" I said, while doing my happy dance.*

*"Damn bitch, how you get to fuck both of them?" Stephanie asked, referring to Chris and Phat. See, they don't know that I've been fucking them both since we all lived in that Co Ed group home. I only met Alisha and Stephanie a few years ago, and we clicked instantly. We often fuck these niggas together. Well, any nigga with money they bring and anyone I bring other than Chris or Phat. I love them niggas and I already have to share Phat with Alexis' stuck up ass, so I'm not trying to introduce their dicks to these bitches.*

*I spotted Phat as soon as he turned the corner to come on our block. "Damn bitch, let me join in," Stephanie damn near begged.*

*"Bitch, you know what's up with that one, so don't play! Plus, he sounded a little stress and I know exactly how to relieve that," I said to Stephanie.*

*"Come on," he said, as he walked past us like he owned the place, making my panties wet in the process.*

*I wasted no time unbuckling his jeans and snatching them down. I took his whole dick in my mouth, making sure I deep throated him every time. I kept forcing his dick deeper and deeper, testing my gag reflexes, while making my mouth wetter. I sucked his dick like I needed him in my life forever because I do. I continued to suck him until he came down my throat.*

*I stood to my feet and lead him down the hall and into my room. "Bitch, I am not getting on that bed!" he snapped at me, stopping me dead in my tracks.*

*"What's with ya'll and fucking in beds?" I asked because him nor Chris won't fuck me in their beds. Most of the time, I catch them slipping and we can fuck in my bed but they act like I don't wash my sheets or something. Yes, I'm fucking more than just them but it's special with them. With everybody else, it's just about the money. I wouldn't dare fuck Phat or Chris on dirty covers.*

*"We talking or fucking?" he asked and I could tell he was getting aggravated. I for damn sure wanted to fuck but shit, if we couldn't get in the bed, I didn't know where he would want to fuck at. "Shit, the floor is better than the bed," he said, slightly pissing me off. I know this nigga don't think the damn floor is cleaner than my bed! I thought to myself.*

*Instead of responding, I stripped down to nothing and laid down on the floor. I watched Phat check his phone then follow suit. My pussy got wetter with each article of clothing that fell off his body. He grabbed a condom and I spread my legs, giving him a great shot of my freshly waxed pussy. He licked his lips at the sight, but I knew he wouldn't dare eat me out. It's fine though because plenty of niggas eat this pussy like it's their last meal.*

*He hovered over me as he slid into me. I moaned out in pleasure and pain as it took me a minute to adjust to his size. Phat has the biggest dick I've ever had, and I've had plenty of dicks. He stroked me slowly and I got wetter and wetter. I could feel my pussy juices sliding down the crack of my ass as Phat gave me long deep strokes. I could feel his dick twitch inside of me, so I knew he was about to cum. I hadn't nutted yet but it's fine because right now, it's all about him.*

*He came and fell on top of me with his dick still in me. "That was so good," I said because even though I didn't cum, he*

*seemed more in tune with me this time than he ever has before.*
*He rolled off of me and my eyes lit up at the sight of the condom*
*rolled up at the base of his dick, letting me know the condom*
*broke. That means he came all in me! I couldn't wait for him to*
*leave, so I could prop my legs up and I did just that.*

Hearing my door slam brought me back to reality. I knew what I
was doing when I straddled him knowing he didn't have a
condom on. Him wearing a condom didn't matter to me because
his and Phat's gifts were welcome in me. I got up naked and ran
after him but it proved to be of no use. I've been noticing that
crazy girl Vanessa hanging around more but she didn't have
Chris wrapped like Alexis has Phat. Thinking about Vanessa, if
she's Chris' girlfriend, I can't have his baby because that bitch
does not play the radio!

I'm not scared of anyone but I'm not a fool. My first day
meeting her she hit me so fucking hard, I saw stars right before I
hit the floor. I couldn't do anything but thank God that she didn't
keep hitting me. That night, I fucked Phat, and my girls and I
walked around there trying to be messy; I forgot about her until I
saw her. Shit, I don't want no beef with her and now I got it. It's
a good thing I don't have to face her alone though. We jumped
her and kicked her ass but I felt like she was holding back. I just
don't know why.

**Vanessa**

Waking up in my bed almost made me think everything that happened was just a dream. My daddy didn't really know I kill people for a living, he didn't bring us Steve to kill, and my mom is still dead and not trying to kill me! Hope quickly faded away as I heard Chris talking to the others in the living room. I climbed out of bed and made my way to where everyone else was.

"What we gone do about this?" Chris asked, as I made my way down the hall. No one knew I was standing there. I watched as everyone appeared to be lost in their own thoughts. "Do anybody know who it was or why they did it?" Chris asked and I could tell from his tone and body language that they were pissing him off. When I glanced at Frankie, I could see she was crying from my position against the wall. "Man, chill out with all that crying shit Frank! Them tears ain't gone change shit; the fuck you crying for? Chris snapped, looking at Frankie. I agreed with everything he said but anybody with eyes can see Frankie's dealing with something. Frankie didn't respond to him. She cried harder.

"It was my mom," I said, stepping into view. I noticed the looks everyone shot in my direction but I also know what I saw!

"Man, that's bullshit! I went to the funeral with you!" Alexis jumped up yelling. The tears running down her face broke my heart. This is my best friend and I understand she's hurting, but I know what I saw! I know what I heard! Someone asked her if they should go ahead and kill me, and she said no! That means she's coming back.

"There's no way that's your mama Vanessa, she's dead! She had an open casket funeral; I remember!" Alexis yelled in my face. My blood began to boil and I wanted to slap fire from her flip mouth right now.

"We probably imagined it was her Lexi; I was only eight," I said, fighting back tears. I was so mad, I wanted to cry and kill everybody. Nobody had my back right now and that's what I needed. The woman I loved with all my heart that I thought was dead is alive and trying to kill me. On top of that, I have no idea why.

"No, you imagined it was today!" Alexis snapped with so much bass in her voice, I was literally talking myself out of hitting her at this moment.

"Ya'll going back and forth like your daddy ain't sitting right here! Ask him!" Chris snapped, causing me to whip my head in the direction of my dad. He was looking at Chris like he wanted to kill him himself.

"Karen's dead baby girl," my daddy said to me while shaking his head.

"See!" Alexis said, pointing towards my dad. "I know you wish she wasn't but she is," she continued, attempting to wrap her arms around me.

I pushed her with all of my might before storming off to my room. I slammed the room door and hopped on the bed. I jumped up like I hadn't just laid across the bed and began to pace the floor. "They don't know what I saw," I said to myself. "I'll show them. My mom is alive and now I have to kill her before she kills us all," I said to myself. "But how?!" I screamed as I dropped down to my knees on the floor.

I sat on my knees and cried as my sobs rocked my body. I felt slender arms wrap around my body in a comforting way and I didn't fight it. I continued to cry until my work phone started ringing. When I stood up, I was shocked to see it was Frankie and not Alexis. "Wait! We need to talk," I said to Frankie, who stood to leave.

"Hello?" I answered.

"I got a job for you," the female voice said.

"Who is this?" I asked. Normally, I don't ask. I simply get the information and do the job once the payment is in my account. This time, there was something familiar about this voice.

"I dropped the list off at your front door. Just call me boss lady. I have a list I need you to take care of and after that, we can meet. You will have your chance to ask me anything you want. Plus, you get Steve back," boss lady said to me, then disconnected the call.

I stood there with tears forming in my eyes with my mouth wide open. "What's wrong?" Frankie asked. I took off running to the front door.

"What the fuck?" I heard Phat say as I ran past them and opened the door. There was a box on the welcome home mat. I grabbed it and brought it inside. "Where did that come from?" Phat asked.

"My mom. She just called me," I said and Alexis sucked her teeth while rolling her eyes.

"Don't make me knock them bitches out yo head! Roll em again!" I snapped, getting pissed off. Frankie came walking slowly out the room.

"Who was that on the phone?" Frankie asked.

"Somebody called her, forreal?" Alexis asked Frankie, like I was lying.

"Bitch, do you think I delivered myself this box?" I asked, snapping on Alexis again. I think she wants me to go upside her fucking head. Maybe she forgot who the fuck I am! Alexis sucked her teeth before flopping down on the couch with her arms folded.

"What if my mom is the lady in the cab that's been following us!" I exclaimed.

"Didn't we establish your mom is dead already," Chris said, walking through the front door. "No, you and that bitch over there said she was dead but I know what I saw, and I know who called me!" I snapped as I looked between Chris and Alexis.

"Wait what? Yo mama called you?" Chris asked with this confused look on his face.

"YES NIGGA!" I screamed. Everyone gave me the side eye as I began to dance. "So, check this out. Me and Frankie were in my room when she called my work phone. She basically told me she has a list of people she wants me to kill then we can have Steve back. She said I'll get a chance to meet with her and ask her whatever I need to ask her after all of this is completed," I said, giving them a run through. Phat looked a bit skeptical until I began to cut open the box in front of them.

"I don't trust this bitch," Chris stated, taking a seat.

"Me either. After we get Steve back, we have to kill her," I said as I opened the box.

"Hold on a second Nessa! You've gone your whole life thinking she was dead and now that you know she isn't, you want to kill her?" Alexis asked, sitting on the edge of the couch.

"Exactly," I answered plainly, pulling out pictures and spreading them out across the coffee table.

"What the fuck is wrong with you, Nessa?" Alexis asked.

"No bitch, what the fuck is wrong with you?! Why shouldn't I kill her? Give me one good reason," I said, as I placed my hands across my chest.

"Because she is your mother!" Alexis screamed.

"Did that stop the bitch from faking her death? Or letting me grow up thinking she was dead? Or throwing a grenade in a room that I was in? The fucking grenade could have killed me! or YOU! or Phat, Chris, Frankie or even my damn Daddy!" I snapped, staring a mud hole in Alexis.

"Ok Nessa," Alexis said, finally understanding where I'm coming from. There were ten pictures all numbered.

"What's with the numbers?" Frankie asked, as I was looking into the box.

"Tape recorders," I said, pouring the tape recorders on the table. Chris grabbed each one and sat them with the picture it corresponded with.

"Let's listen to the first four tapes and execute a plan," I suggested, before grabbing the picture of a dark skinned fat man. I grabbed the tape recorder and pressed play.

"Hey Sweetheart! If you're listening to this, then you have received the package. You should be looking at a fat, black bag of shit! His name is John Abrams and he works down at Merchants Bank. He was one of my accountants. I just found out he's been skimming off the top. I want him dead for $50,000. I'll give you an extra $1,000 for each finger you cut off." The tape ended.

"Wow," Alexis said, as she shook her head.

"I can't believe this shit. Your moms did all of this to hire you to kill people," Phat said. I grabbed a pen and paper and wrote down everything I knew about John Abrams and what I need to find out.

I grabbed the next tape numbered two. "Nessie baby, no need to get ahead of yourself. Take care of John Abrams while he's still in town, then come back to her. Let's do this one at a time. After each job is complete, I'll deposit the funds in your account. Press pause," boss lady said over the recorder.

I pressed pause. "How did she know I would listen to more than just the first one?" I said out loud to myself. Everyone grew quiet but I needed to prep, so I could go and get this job over with. The faster I killed John Abrams, the faster I could move on to the next one until I completed the list. Then I'll get the sweet pleasure of killing mommy dearest.

## Boss Lady

I don't quite know how to feel after seeing Michael after all of these years! I can't believe I still love him after all I've been through because of him and that bitch, Vanessa. I'm going to kill her just to hurt Michael! She's no child of mine anyway! I have one child, a son, and I can't even say I'm proud of what he's become. Fucking weakling!

Vanessa is far stronger than I would have given her credit for and under different circumstances, I'd want her to be a part of my team. Unfortunately for her, her dog ass daddy is the reason she has to die. I plan on making her help me before I take her out though. Hell, I'm going to play around with her first. I have quite a few people that I need dead for various reasons.

"Boss lady," Aurel, my Slovakian guard, said, snapping me out of my thoughts.

"Yes," I said, turning around to face him. Aurel is the only person I trust with my life. He's my tall glass of Slovakian milk! He's 6'2" with deep blue eyes, a muscular build, and a 9" dick to die for! Yes, I've had the pleasure of bouncing, bobbing, and weaving on it whenever we get the chance.

"Branko informed me prisoner was drugged. Can't move," Aurel said to me, causing my face to twist up in anger.

"What the fuck did they give him?" I asked, picking up a shot glass. I poured myself a shot of patron, downed it, and poured another one.

"A paralyzing agent," Aurel answered, watching me closely. *Where the fuck did they get that?* I thought to myself.

I need to go ahead and get her to do what I need her to do then kill her, so I can move on with my life. If Michael would not have hurt me so bad, I wouldn't kill his daughter but we can't change our past. We can run from it or learn from it, and it's time that Michael learns from it. "Get my phone for me please," I said, slightly demanding Aurel to get my phone. It doesn't matter how good his dick, I'm still the boss. I have very few Americans working for me. Most of my team is made up of Slovakian soldiers. Funny thing is, all of the people that has crossed me are American!

"Hello?" Vanessa answered and I cringed at the sound of her voice.

"I got a job for you," I said into the receiver. I motioned for Aurel to come closer as I continued my conversation while removing my clothes.

"Who is this?" Vanessa asked and I rolled my eyes at the dumb question. She's had a few jobs, but they're all sent by the same guy. Considering what just happened, she should assume it's me.

"I dropped the list off at your front door. Just call me boss lady. I have a list I need you to take care of and after that, we can meet. You will have your chance to ask me anything you want. Plus, you get Steve back," I said as Aurel covered my pussy with his mouth. I inhaled deeply as I hung the phone up.

"Fuck!" I yelled out. The only noise that could be heard was Aurel smacking on this pussy and my moans. "Do that shit Aurel!" I said as my body began to convulse. He continued slurping until my intense convulsions turned into a slight shake. He stood to his face and looked directly into my eyes, waiting on my next command. I love the relationship we have because I'm in total control and he never steps out of his lane. This relationship is the complete opposite of the one I shared with Michael years and years ago.

"I want the Slovakian punishment," I said with a voice filled with lust. The Slovakian punishment is extremely rough sex! Without saying a word, Aurel grabbed my hair and turned my body in the opposite direction. He bent me over forcefully before smacking my ass. It hurt so good. He grabbed the thin fabric I had on and snatched it off before he threw it on the floor. I could feel my pussy juices sliding down my legs as I prepared to receive my favorite past time.

Aurel tightened his grip on my hair as he plunged himself deep into my walls. I let out a deep monstrous groan as he began to pummel the pussy. I mean, Aurel was beating it up like it stole from him and I couldn't catch my breath. My body began to shake as another orgasm hit me. Aurel smacked my ass then tossed me on the lounge chair. He walked to me slowly with a frown on his face as his dick swayed from side to side.

He forced my legs open. I felt a cool breeze tickle my pussy. I moaned softly. Aurel grabbed my legs where my thighs and hip meets and yanked my ass on the arm of the chair. I knew after this, my neck would have a crook in it. I tried repositioning myself but Aurel slammed his dick into me! "Ahhh! Fuck!" I yelled out. The pain hurt so good; I couldn't take it. I locked my arms around the other arm on the chair, so I could pull myself away from him. Aurel shook his head then clasped his large hands around my waist. He pulled me to him, forcing me to meet every stroke. My body began to shake again. Shortly after I came for the third time, Aurel came. He got dressed and exited, just as quickly as he entered.

It took me about fifteen minutes before I could stand and even then, my legs were still wobbly. I managed to draw myself a hot bath. I laid in the tub thinking of all the money I was about to make and all the pain I was about to cause.

After my bath, I hopped on my elevator and went to the ground floor where my prisoner was located. "I see you're able to move your limbs on your own," I said, walking to the living room area. Steve sat watching TV like he was home and not in danger.

"Yes ma'am," he replied, without taking his eyes off the TV. I glanced over at the TV to see what had his attention and he was watching that show called Breaking Bad.

"Do you have any questions for me?" I asked as I took a seat next to him.

**Steve**

It took hours for me to finally be able to use my legs and arms, but they were still wobbly. I climbed off the table and fell to the floor. My legs were extremely weak. I crawled to the wall, so I could use it to stand to my feet. Once I got my balance, I walked through the living quarters, occasionally using the wall for support.

To the left of the elevator is a hallway. I walked down the hallway and came to two bedrooms. Everything everywhere was black. I'd never seen black carpet before and it looked nice. I left out of the rooms and headed passed the elevator. The kitchen was directly in front of the elevator and had all black appliances. Next, there was the living room, which had the only TV that I've seen so far. I walked through the living room and found a bathroom, then a home gym, and the last room looked like a yoga room. Those flat mats covered the entire floor and of course, they were black.

I heard the elevator chime, so I walked as fast as possible to the living room. I turned the TV on as I sat on the couch and began watching. I could feel her powerful presence getting closer to me. She commanded attention but I refuse to give her any.

"I see you're able to move your limbs on your own," she said as she closed in on me.

"Yes ma'am," I said, without looking away from the TV. I didn't want to look at her because I don't know exactly what sets her off. Hell, what if I look at her and she gets mad because I looked at her and kill me? I continued watching the TV, although I had no idea what I was looking at.

"Do you have any questions for me?" she asked, sitting right next to me.

I closed my eyes as I inhaled her scent. I hadn't been this close to a woman in so long. I could feel my dick growing in my pants, so I repositioned my body so she wouldn't see it. She laughed softly before moving to the other couch. "I must say I have an effect on men but that's a first," she said laughing. I laughed with her.

"It's been a while. A long while," I said, without looking at her.

"So, any questions?" she asked, crossing her legs. I sighed deeply as my eyes developed a mind of their own, traveling all over her body. She cleared her throat snapping me back to my current predicament.

"Am I locked in down here?" I asked, causing her to laugh.

"Baby, none of my doors have a lock option. You can roam all over my estate. You just can't leave out the gate," she explained, letting me know I am a prisoner. I'd rather be here than with Vanessa though.

"How long are you going to keep me?" I asked her.

"Until Vanessa finishes what I've assigned her to do," she stated simply.

"Ya'll made a deal or something? What is it?" I asked.

I could feel my heart rate picking up speed as I waited for her to answer. "A deal? Naw, more like an offer she couldn't refuse. I asked her to do me a favor. To make it sweet, I'm going to pay and once the job is complete, she gets you," she said with a shrug of the shoulders.

"She's going to kill me," I said with worry evident in my voice.

"That's neither here nor there," she stated, as she uncrossed and re-crossed her long legs.

"Who are you?" I asked.

"Boss Lady," she said, as she stood to leave.

"Are you her mother?" I yelled from the couch once she made it to the elevator door.

She stopped in her tracks without turning around. "I only have a son," she said, before stepping into the elevator.

I sat on the couch, even more confused than I was before she came in here in the first place. I don't want to die but I don't know what to do to live. I tried replaying our brief conversation but nothing was adding up. I know what I heard back at the warehouse. I know I heard Vanessa call her mom! I know Vanessa's dad has three kids: Michael, Vanessa and Princess. Boss Lady is saying she only has a son. Maybe she's only Wayne's mother but helped raise Vanessa and Princess.

"What favor is Vanessa doing and how long will it take?" I asked myself out loud. I stood to my feet and began pacing the floor. "I don't know what to do! Fuck!" I yelled. The elevator chimed and I quickly sat back down. The Slovakian body guard came strolling out of the elevator like he lives here.

"You want tour?" he asked in that weird accent. I shook my head no in response. All I want to do is go back in time and not cross them to begin with. At least, then I wouldn't have Vanessa to worry about. If I could get out of here, then I could find Vanessa and kill her first. She's now the leader and if I take out the head, the body will fall.

**Chris**

Confusion was an understatement for what I felt walking into the house hearing them talk about Vanessa's dead ass mama! Sorry, not sorry! I believe people that die should stay dead! Hell, you died for a reason and that was not to come back from the dead and kill your damn daughter!

"What if my mom is the lady in the cab that's been following us!" I heard Vanessa shout as I walked through the door.

I shook my head at all of the bullshit I'm encountering today. "Didn't we establish your mom is dead already," I said, closing the door behind me. I know I sound insensitive but fuck that shit! Either her mom is dead or she ain't. Ain't no way she saw her mom in the casket and now she's back. No, the bitch is still buried six feet deep.

"No, you and that bitch over there said she was dead but I know what I saw, and I know who called me!" Vanessa snapped, looking at Alexis then back at me. I don't know what them two have going on but they need to fix that shit before Casper come back.

"Wait, what? Yo mama called you?" I asked, once I realized what her crazy ass just said. This shit just keeps getting better and better.

"YES NIGGA!" she screamed like I'm the crazy one. Everybody looked at her crazy but I know what she needs. All she needs is some dick in her life and she will forget all about her mama, and we can figure out who this bitch really is.

"So, check this out. Me and Frankie were in my room when she called my work phone. She basically told me she has a list of people she wants me to kill, then we can have Steve back. She said I'll get a chance to meet with her and ask her whatever I need to ask her after all of this is completed," Vanessa said and I was literally standing there with my mouth open. Shit is unbelievable! There's no possible way her mom is alive! Hell, even her daddy told her that her mom is dead. She began to cut open a box and I was really looking crazy. I crossed my fingers and toes, in case this is a bomb.

"I don't trust this bitch," I stated, taking a seat.

"Me either. After we get Steve back, we have to kill her," Vanessa said as she opened the box. I totally agree with that.

"Hold on a second Nessa! You've gone your whole life thinking she was dead and now that you know she isn't, you want to kill her?" Alexis asked, scooting to the end of the couch like she was about to do something.

"Exactly," Vanessa answered, as she pulled out pictures and spread them out across the coffee table.

"What the fuck is wrong with you, Nessa?" Alexis asked.

"No bitch, what the fuck is wrong with you?! Why shouldn't I kill her? Give me one good reason," Vanessa said, as she placed her arms across her chest. I know when black women do that move, they ready to fight. Either that or place their hands on their hips. I looked over at Phat but I guess he was waiting on her to answer.

"Because she is your mother!" Alexis screamed, making no sense at all. *No her mother is dead!* I thought to myself.

"Did that stop the bitch from faking her death? Or letting me grow up thinking she was dead? Or throwing a grenade in a room that I was in? The fucking grenade could have killed me! or YOU! or Phat, Chris, Frankie or even my damn Daddy!" Vanessa snapped, like she wanted to snap Alexis' neck.

"Ok Nessa," Alexis said. I don't know if she finally gets it or if she finally gave up. Vanessa laid ten pictures across the table and I noticed they were numbered, so I put them in numerical order.

"What's with the numbers?" Frankie asked, while Vanessa looked in the box.

"Tape recorders," Vanessa said, pouring the tape recorders on table. I grabbed each tape recorder and placed each one on top of the picture it corresponded with. "Let's listen to the first four tapes and execute a plan," Vanessa suggested, before grabbing the picture of a dark skinned fat man. She grabbed the tape recorder and pressed play.

"Hey Sweetheart! If you're listening to this, then you have received the package. You should be looking at a fat, black bag of shit! His name is John Abrams and he works down at Merchants Bank. He was one of my accountants. I just found out he's been skimming off the top. I want him dead for $50,000. I'll give you an extra $1,000 for each finger you cut off." The tape ended.

"Wow," Alexis said, as she shook her head. Shit, I was shaking my head too but not for the reason everyone else was. Hell, her mom is about to pay her $50,000 to kill someone. That's a lot of fucking money.

"I can't believe this shit. Your moms did all of this to hire you to kill people," Phat said. Vanessa grabbed a pen and paper and began writing some shit down but I couldn't see the paper.

She grabbed the next tape numbered two. "Nessie baby, no need to get ahead of yourself. Take care of John Abrams while he's still in town, then come back to her. Let's do this one at a time. After each job is complete, I'll deposit the funds in your account.

Press pause," Casper said over the recorder. Yes, I'm going to call this bitch Casper!

Vanessa pressed pause with her face frowned up. "How did she know I would listen to more than just the first one?" Vanessa asked, like we were supposed to know. She got up and walked out of the room after nobody responded to her.

"Yall think she will be ok?" Alexis asked.
"Shit, she thought she lost her mom when she was kid. She just found out that her mom is alive. Well possibly. And that she's trying to kill her. This will either make her stronger or fuck her up mentally," I said with a shrug of the shoulders.

Frankie rolled her eyes at me then sucked her teeth. Phat shook his head and laughed. "Gone and check on her nigga; you know you want to," Phat said, still laughing at me.

"Man, I ain't got my ass on that girl," I said, heading to my room to hop in the shower before I went to check on Vanessa. The way she smelled Phat from a distance; I know I need to shower first. All I got was some head but she may smell a bitch breath or something. After I took my shower, I walked in her room without knocking.

She looked so beautiful sitting on her bed, writing in a notebook. She had reading glasses on and her hair pulled up in a bun that was falling out the rubber band. Her legs were crossed slightly as she leaned against the headboard for support. "What you doing?" I asked, as I closed in on the bed. She stuck the top of the pen slightly in her mouth as she looked at me over the rim of her glasses, and I wanted to say fuck all of this shit we have going on right now and fuck her silly.

"You just gone stare at me all day or help?" she asked.

"Help with what?" I asked, causing her to laugh. I hadn't heard shit she just said to me. I guess I zoned out.

"I said I'm trying to figure out as much as I can about John Abrams, so we can get this money and move on to the next one. Then, I asked if you were going to help," she said with a smile. I walked closer to her and kissed her forehead. When I pulled away, she had her eyes closed. I smiled and climbed on the bed but she pushed me off.

"What the fuck girl?" I asked, remembering the last time I called her a bitch, it didn't end well. We were both bruised the fuck up, me with more bruises than her. I don't fight women. I just stole on her a few times when she would hit me too hard.

"Take your damn jeans off," she said with her face balled up in anger. She lets the smallest things piss her off but it's so funny to me. Had I worn sweatpants in here, she wouldn't have mind me climbing in her bed but she hates people getting in her bed with jeans. I have no idea why.

I slipped out of my jeans and hopped on the bed. "So, where do we start?" I asked, as I reached for the notebook.

"Um, you start by putting that thing away," she said, as she pointed between my legs. She scooted to the other side of the bed with fear written on her face.

*This bitch really is a virgin*, I thought to myself. I laughed and adjusted my boxers, so it would fall back in. "Ok, where do I start?" I asked again.

"I want to try to figure out where and how to kill him," she said.

"Well, it has to be in a private setting because I have to cut his fingers off," she said in deep thought. She didn't need me here but I wasn't going anywhere.

I sat on the bed watching her think to herself before jotting down a few notes. She looked stunning. She repositioned her body, so she was laying down as she wrote. Every so often, a piece of hair would fall from behind her ear and she would swipe it back behind it. I felt invisible as I watched her work. She placed the pen top on her bottom lip and when her tongue danced across it, I couldn't help myself.

## Vanessa

I walked swiftly out of the living room, so I could go in my room to brainstorm. I desperately needed to find a way to kill this man and get his fingers in a timely manner. I need her dead like yesterday and the only way I could do that was to kill off all ten people on her list. Then, she will give me Steve and I'll let Chris and Phat handle him while I handle her. Hopefully, we can meet alone because I'm pretty sure I can take her. All I want to know is why. Why did she fake her death? Did she really have breast cancer? Was she really sick or was it a part of her exit strategy?

I climbed on my bed, grabbed my composition notebook, and wrote John Abrams across the top of the first sheet. Underneath his name, I wrote everything she told me about him on the tape. I began to jot down ways to get to him when Chris made his presence known in my room. Sometimes, I can hardly look at him because he's a major distraction. Chris is so sexy and my problem is he knows it. He looks at me like I'm a plate of food and he's ready to eat every time he sees me. He's in here offering his help but he's not really helping.

After his dick slipped through his pee hole in his boxers, I damn near jumped out of my own damn bed. If I wasn't scared to have sex before, I definitely am now. I like Chris, I like him a lot but he's still fucking off, and I don't want to get distracted from my work. I don't think I'm capable of loving anyone, so I don't have to worry about him hurting me. What I have to worry about is my anger causing me to kill people recklessly and I go to jail behind some emotional shit. I'm not trying to get locked up behind no nigga. I know Chris still fucks with Brittany heavily and she's too bold for me. I already owe her and her little friends a good ass whooping.

I laid across my bed, executing the perfect plan to catch John Abrams slipping. All of a sudden, Chris leaned over and pushed the notebook on the floor. "What the-," I started but Chris cut me off when he pressed his lips against mine. He kissed me deeply as his hands roamed my entire body hungrily. He slid my jogging pants and panties off while kissing me. I wanted to protest but I didn't want him to stop kissing me. He grabbed my t-shirt and ripped it open. He unclasped my bra and pulled it off. He never once broke our kiss.

He planted soft kisses down between my breast. He stopped to give attention to my nipples. My body tingled as he sucked one while pinching the other. Then he switched! I didn't know what I was feeling but everything he was doing was feeling way better than what he did last time. He kissed his way down my stomach before sticking his tongue in my belly button. My back arched itself, probably from the pleasure. I don't know. I just laid there and let Chris have his way with my body.

He kissed and sucked on my inner thighs as he opened my legs slightly. He blew his breath lightly between my legs before he started sucking on my pearl. He was sucking and slurping and I was moaning like crazy. Even he was moaning and I had no idea why. I felt a tingling feeling that started at my toes. I tried to stop it by balling them up as tight as possible but it didn't work. I felt the feeling travel up my legs as my heart started to beat faster. I'd never been more afraid of anything in my life!

I grabbed Chris's head pushing him away but it only made him suck harder. "Ahhh! Gosh Stop! Chris Stop! Please!" I yelled panting. He ignored my pleas as he continued to suck and slurp. My body started trembling as he stuck his tongue inside of me. I tried flipping my body over but he locked my legs down with his arms. I was stuck! I couldn't move! I was about to die! Then it hit me! A wave of ecstasy! Chris opened my floodgates and they poured. My whole body shook and he continued to lap up my juices.

It took several minutes before my breathing was under control again. Chris had positioned his body over mine as he stared into my eyes. "Are you really a virgin?" he asked with a serious look on his face. I nodded my response. "Do you trust me?" he asked. I nodded my response. "It's only going to hurt for a little while," he said. My heart started beating hard in my chest.

I could feel the head at my opening. He started kissing me slowly as he slid the head in. It burned slightly but I fought through it. A tear escaped. Chris kissed it away. That gesture caused more tears to fall. "Do you want me to stop?" he asked. I shook my head no. He rotated his hips, easing himself deeper and deeper into me. It hurt like hell and I kept sliding away from him. He slid his arm under my back before lifting my body and rotating it. It slid deeper and I began to wonder when would deep ever be deep enough. I continued to slide away from him until I hit the headboard.

I punched him in the chest. "Stop running," he said, smiling. He kissed me deeply as he pushed all of him in me with one thrust. I gasped in his mouth. He released a deep breath in mine. He continued to move in and out of me at a slow pace and the wetter I got, the better it felt. Before long, my body was shaking again. This time I didn't fight it. He was no longer kissing me. He had his face buried in the crook of my neck as he moved in and out of me. I could feel his hot breath on my neck as he continued to move slowly. He started winding his hips in me and I was going crazy and scratching his back because it felt so good.

"Fuck! Chris! Shit!" I moaned out, trying to catch my breath.

"You feel so fuckin good baby," he whispered in my ear, making me wetter. He pulled back and stared in my eyes as he made love to my mind, body, and soul.

I could feel his dick jump inside of me as I felt that all too familiar tingle starting at my toes. He could no longer make eye contact. His eyes rolled in the back of his head as we came together. "I love you," he said. I had my eyes closed, so I pretended to be asleep.

The fact of the matter is I don't think I'm capable of loving anyone.


## Chris

I knew I loved Vanessa before I told her. Shit, I knew I loved her the first day I met her. She's different. I honestly thought she was lying about being a virgin though. I made love to her for the first time in my life. I have never made love to anyone. It's normally straight fucking with me but I've never felt like this about anyone. I knew she was really a virgin from the fear behind her eyes when my dick fell out my boxers. Shit, I was about to let her finish mapping out her plan but I couldn't. I wanted to feel her.

Now that I've felt her, I left my mark and the feelings I gave her would be hard to come by. Brittany can consider herself cut the fuck off. Shit, I can teach Vanessa what to do by telling her what I like. She can watch YouTube or something, hell. I got everything I need right here in this bed. That's why I came all in her. She's made enough money to chill the fuck out after this and let me be a man and keep stacking. She can kick back and let me make her happy.

My next plan is to start taking these people out that's on the list her mom gave her. I'm still on the fence about her mom being alive. I don't think her dad would have put her through everything she's been through with losing a mother if she hadn't really lost one. Plus, he just told her that her mom is dead and I believe him. I don't know what's going but I know I'm going to find out.

I made her body cum so much; she fell asleep afterwards. I couldn't believe myself when I told her I love her but I'm glad I did. The things I was about to do will definitely show her I'm down for the cause. I grabbed her backpack and notebook and headed out on a mission. I stopped in the living room and grabbed the picture of John Abrams.

"Where you going?" Phat asked before I reached the door.

"I'm on a mission," I said, looking back at him. He looked at Alexis. She nodded back at him and he followed me out the door. "Man, yo ass whipped," I said laughing, once we got inside the truck.

"Nigga, I heard ya'll in there. You bout to understand exactly how I feel," he said, laughing. I thought about what just happened and how I felt while it was happening.

"You right," I said, laughing with him.

I pulled out the yard and headed down to the bank. "What time is it?" Phat asked.

"4:30. The bank close in 30 minutes so by the time we get there, he should be locking up. We can follow him home," I said, not putting much thought into the plan at all.

"What if his family is there?" Phat asked, looking at me sideways.

"Then they will die with him," I said with my face frowned up. I didn't ask Phat to come and if he's going to punk out, then he need to tell me now before he fuck me up later with a change of heart.

"You done?" I asked, without taking my eyes off the road.

"Let's do this shit, so I can get back to my girl. Shit, the faster we kill these people, the faster we get to Steve's ass," Phat said, reminding me of our ultimate goal. I know for Vanessa it's killing her mom but for us, it's our brother.

We pulled up to the bank but couldn't find a parking spot. We circled the block for about 10 minutes before we noticed this guy pulling out of a spot near the door. "That's him," Phat said, pointing at the car getting ready to pull out of the spot.

We followed him for about an hour before we pulled up to this nice brownstone. There was a sign in the yard with the letter A on it. I watched him climb out of his 2015 Cadillac and walk up to the front door. A chunky lady met him at the door with her hands on her hips and a frown on her fat face. He threw his hands in the air in exasperation. "How we gone get in?" Phat asked, since neither of us are good at picking locks.

"I guess we're winging it. Make sure your phone on silent," I said, getting out the truck we drove. Phat checked his phone then hopped out the truck.

We made our way to the front door and the yelling could be heard before we got on the porch. I used my shirt to turn the doorknob and couldn't believe it was open. We crept inside, closing the door behind us. "Nobody's watching you Helen! I told you I got us covered!" John yelled at his wife.

"I'm telling you, she's following me and I know she's following you too! We shouldn't have taken her money," she said with tears streaming down her face.

"She's right. You shouldn't have," I said, stepping into view.

"Uh uh!" Phat said, right before his wife was about to scream.

"Where's the money?" I asked, looking directly at John.

"Under the sofa cushion," he said with his head hanging low.

"Under the sofa cushion?" Phat and I asked simultaneously. Out of all the places to hide large sums of money, he chooses to pick the place people check off top. I walked over to their couch and lifted the cushions. Low and behold, twelve stacks of money lined neatly under the cushion. I walked into the kitchen to get a garbage bag and filled it with the money. I searched the entire house for more money but didn't find any.

"Ok Bro, we're clear," I said to Phat. He nodded his head, then shot Helen and John between their eyes. Neither of them had a chance to scream before the bullet struck them.

"Let's go," Phat said, turning on the balls of his feet.

"Wait man, we have to get his fingers," I said, grabbing the back of shirt. "You get one hand and I'll get the other one." I grabbed two of the sharpest blades I saw in Vanessa's bag and handed one off to Phat. The blade was so sharp that I was able to cut two fingers off at a time. It took us no time to cut all of his fingers off. I threw them in a grocery bag and we left out the house the same way we came.

"Think we should set the house on fire?" Phat asked.

"If you want to, since we weren't in there long, we have time to spare," I answered him. This nigga grabbed a tank of gasoline out the back like he's been waiting on his chance to burn some shit up. "Nigga!" I said, laughing as we got out of the car. Phat joined in. We haven't hung out like this in a minute. Maybe after we kill all these mufuckers, we can take a trip somewhere or something.

We walked back through the front door. Phat poured gasoline only in the rooms we were in, started the fire, and we were out.

He had the biggest smile on his face, reminding me of why he used to stay in trouble in the group home. Phat's ass use to set tissue on fire in the bathroom sink all the time. One day, he dropped it before he made it to the sink and the shower curtain caught fire. I ran in the bathroom behind him with a towel and it caught on fire.

"What you laughing for?" Phat asked.

"Man, do you remember when you set the whole bathroom on fire and everything I grabbed trying to put it out caught on fire too?" I asked, as I laughed harder.

"Man, hell yea! That shit was so crazy!" Phat said laughing.

"Man, they beat our ass with them paddles like I helped you start the fire," I said.

"Nigga, you helped keep it going though," he said laughing.

SCREECH! An all-black van pulled in front of us. I slammed on the brakes, threw the car in reverse, and headed in the opposite direction until I was able to turn around. "What the fuck?!" Phat yelled, grabbing his gun. He hung his body out the window and shot into the windshield. I guess he hit the driver because the whole van swerved off the road. "Shit!" Phat said, climbing back inside the truck. I looked in rearview mirror and saw another van pull behind us.

BOOM! They rear ended us. "Take em out!" I yelled. Phat hung his body back out the window but a barrage of bullets sent his way made him jump back inside.

"Fuck!" he said, panting heavily. BOOM! They rear ended us again and I lost control of the wheel. It took me a few minutes and I side swiped some cars that were parked but I was able to gain control. Phat was crawling back out the window but I pulled him back in. "What you doing?" he asked, mugging me.

"Man, Alexis and Vanessa gone kill me if they kill you! Fuck it, let them catch us and we shoot them when they get closer," I said, looking at him.

"Alright man, just watch the road," he said, right as we were rear ended again. I turned the wheel as hard as I could, leading us down a side road. I looked in the rear view mirror and they crashed into a car that was parked on the corner. I hit another left and hopped on the highway headed back home. I wanted to pull over, so we could steal a car, since our truck was fucked up but Phat didn't want to chance them catching up to us if we stopped to steal a car.

It took us about an hour and a half to get home because I passed the exit and had to turn around. When we pulled up, I couldn't believe my eyes. There were four black vans parked out front.

**Vanessa**

I played sleep until I heard my room door open then close. I opened my eyes but I was extremely tired. It felt like I had been drugged. I felt so good and relaxed. The only thing that hurt was between my legs. I crawled out of bed just to shower before I climbed back in my bed. Then, I drifted off to sleep.

"Aaaaaahhhh!" I heard someone screaming from the living room. I grabbed my phone and noticed I had been asleep for almost two hours. I called my dad.

"Are you ok baby girl?" he asked, answering his phone.

"No daddy, someone is in the house. I hear screaming from my room," I said in a hushed tone. I slid my body out of bed to get my backpack but I couldn't find it. "My backpack is missing," I said into the phone. "Daddy, are you still there?" I asked, once I realized he hadn't responded.

"Yes, I'm on my way," he said without hanging up. I searched all over my room for a weapon but came up short.

"Shit!" I said out loud.

"Language," my daddy said, like I don't have the right to curse right now. People are in the house and he's worried about my language. "Nessa," he said sternly.

"Sorry daddy," I said, looking at my bed from the floor. I saw something shiny out of the corner of my eye and when I glanced over at it, I almost screamed. "My sword!" I said, just as my room door flew open.

I sat my phone on the bed and tumbled twice to get to my sword. I brought it down hard, slicing the guy's head smoove off his shoulders. The guy stopped in his tracks, probably because he was shocked. Wrong move. That gave me enough time to jump to my feet. I did a low spin, using my sword to cut his legs at the knees. He screamed out in pain as he hit the floor. I jumped in the air and came down hard with my sword, stabbing him in the neck.

I tumbled to the door and stood to my feet with my back against the wall. I could hear footsteps coming my way but I couldn't step out swinging. I couldn't take the chance of killing one of my people. "Let them be ok God," I said softly.

Another man ran in my room. "Aurel, in here," the guy said with some kind of weird accent. "Boss Lady, no like this," the guy continued as, who I assumed was Aurel, entered my room. I swung the sword with all of my might. It sliced into him at his stomach and went halfway through before getting stuck. He started making gurgling sounds causing Aurel to look at me. I could see the fire behind his eyes, although I couldn't see his face. They all wore masks. I tried pulling my sword out but it only sliced into him deeper, making it harder to pull out.

Aurel kicked me hard as I don't know what, knocking the wind out of me. He kicked me so hard; I hit the wall and fell with the sword in my hand. The top half of the guy's body fell off the bottom half before his legs hit the floor. It was an extremely comical sight. Under different circumstances, I would have laughed. "Nobody trying hurt you," Aurel said in the same accent the other guy used.

"What do you want then?" I asked with a confused expression on my face.

"Money," he said simply.

"I don't know what the fuck you're talking about! I ain't got no damn money. Boss Lady is supposed to pay me!" I snapped as I got up from the floor.

"Yes," he said, pissing me off.

"Yes what?" I asked, making sure I had a nice firm grip on my sword.
"Boss Lady sent money," he said as he walked out the door. I followed him out the room and up the hallway. As soon as we reached the living room, the door was kicked in.

POW! POW! POW!

I hit the floor. Phat came in shooting. He took out three of Boss Lady's men and only stopped because the other one ducked behind Alexis. "They aren't here to hurt us. Boss Lady sent a payment here," I explained, getting up from the floor.

"Bullshit!" Alexis yelled with fire in her eyes. I don't know what the fuck has been going on her with and this attitude but she need to check it.

"Bitch, shut the fuck up! If they wanted us dead, we would all be dead right now but guess what? We're all here and they lost six men," I said with a smirk on my face.

Aurel gave me a weird look. "Boss Lady no like this," he said.

"Boss Lady need a new approach then! She was supposed to deposit the money anyway," I said, rolling my eyes and walking past him. I could feel Chris staring at me but I didn't acknowledge him at all.

"She deposit if you kill alone. You had help, so you split," he said, dumping $60,000 on the coffee table on top of the pictures and tape recorders. I was beyond confused. "You have fingers?" he asked, turning towards the door.

"Yea," Chris said, handing him a bag.

"$30,000 for you and $30,000 for you," Aurel said to Phat and Chris. I looked at Alexis, who had this dumb looking smirk on her face.

"What is that look for?" I asked Alexis.

"What?" she asked, wiping the look off her face. I just nodded my head. See, I take shit in and keep it stored for later. Eventually, things will start adding up and I'll be ready. I just hope if she's against me, she's ready.

Aurel and the only man left walked out the door. "We be back for the others," Aurel said. I watched him hop in a van and back up to my door. Him and the other guy came in and took all of the dead bodies out of our house. "You keep vans," Aurel said, as they pulled off in one of the vans, leaving three of them behind.

After they pulled off, my dad came flying in. I shook my head and took a seat in the Lay-Z-Boy chair. I watched as Phat and

Chris divided their money. They carried their shares to their rooms and came back to join us. Alexis had this crazy grin on her face and Frankie was kind of just there. I need to remember to see what's up with her. She's been acting crazy since I drugged her.

*It was the night Steve and James set all of the shit up, so everyone could be killed but them. Well, at least, I think that's how it went. A guy got in on Frankie's watch, so it was only right that we tortured him in her room. While Chris and I set everything up, I heard a gunshot. I jumped backwards and hit my back on Frankie's dresser. Chris and I shared a quick glance before he knocked the guy out. I jumped up and ran into the living room. There was a guy slumped over in the doorway. I looked at Frankie, who still had the gun aimed at the door. I knew she was shaken up but nobody had time to baby her.*

*I shook my head and walked over to the door, so I could look out of it. I needed to make sure no one else was coming. There was an all-black truck a few buildings over that I hadn't noticed before. I pulled the body in the house. "What the hell happened?" Chris asked, stepping into the living room.*

*"Come help me," I said, trying not to grab my side since it still hurt from Brittany and her friends jumping me outside. Chris picked the guy up and yelled for me to bring a chair into Frankie's room. We had to torture him too, to figure out who sent them in the first place. I needed to check on Frankie first though, especially since she was keeping watch.*

*When I walked back into the living room, Frankie was still sitting in the same spot with the door wide open. I closed the door and took the gun from her. She started crying and rocking herself backwards and forwards. I gave her some tissue but when she started crying harder, I took it back. People think I'm crazy but they must have never witnessed Frankie's behavior after using a gun.*

*I wanted to slap her. You know how they do on TV to snap someone out of a panic, but I decided against it. I crushed up some pain pills and poured them in some juice, then made her drink it. After she fell asleep, I slid the gun in her hands. I knew that if someone burst in here and scared her, she would start shooting. That's exactly what she did. Problem is, she shot Alexis.*

"Vanessa, lemme holla at you," Chris said from the hallway, snapping me back into our present moment. Alexis shot me a look but she didn't say anything. *The fuck is up with her?* I thought to myself. I stood up and followed Chris into his room.

## Boss Lady

"You lost what?!" I screamed at Aurel. My blood was boiling, listening to Aurel give me a run through of what happened when I sent them to pay Vanessa's little stooges for taking out the first target on the list. I was shocked that Vanessa didn't get right on it and I wondered why. Doesn't matter because it got done! They can have an entire hit squad for all I care and it wouldn't make a damn bit of difference, as long as everybody that I need to die is dead! They don't have to know that they will die in the end.

"She attacked. We lost six," Aurel said, putting the blame on Vanessa. I've been watching the little crazy bitch for years, so I knew she would attack. What I didn't know was that my team wouldn't be able to hold up to a little bitch that weighed 120 pounds soaked and wet!

"How did she manage to take out six men?" I asked, trying desperately to calm my nerves because they were on 10!

"She took out three alone. Her friend took out three," Aurel said, without shying away from my gaze.

I could see clearly he didn't fear me and I know that's going to be a problem. In order for my team to obey me without questioning anything, they have to fear me. I need him to fear me! "How the fuck did the little bitch take out three men? Didn't you take eight of my strongest men, including yourself?" I asked, trying to wrap my brain around this.

"A sword," he said, and my mouth hit the floor.

"This bitch took out three of my strongest men with a fucking knife?!" I screamed.

I started to feel dizzy, so I sat on the arm of the lounge chair in my room. "A sword, Boss Lady. She cut one head off. One legs off, then stab in neck. The other one, she cut in half," Aurel said and I could feel the vomit rising from the pit of my stomach. I grabbed my glass of wine off the end table and took a few sips to ease my stomach pain.

"What happened to the other 3?" I asked.

"The grey eyed fellow shot them," he said and I smiled slightly.

These guys went and killed the first target and made it in time to kill three of my men. Maybe I messed up hiring mostly Slovakian soldiers. Maybe I should have just kept it all in the family. It's too late for that though because the only way I can hurt Michael the way he hurt me is to kill Vanessa. A heart for a heart.

## Phat

I've never experienced the kind of rush I've experienced today. Vanessa may be onto something with this hired hit shit. I'm going to have to sit down and talk to her about joining her. The look on Helen and John's face right before I shot them in the head was to die for! Then, to be able to set shit on fire afterwards! Oh yeah, they will be calling me the fireman!

When we left and that van came out of nowhere, I didn't think twice as I climbed out the window and took the driver out. When the other van came and I climbed back out the window, I could see the hail of bullets heading towards me. I jumped back inside but my adrenaline was pumping. My dick was hard from the excitement.

All of the excitement inside of me died when we pulled up and saw those black vans in the yard. "Aye, should we go around back?" Chris asked, throwing the truck in park.

"Hell naw!" I said, jumping out the truck. Chris followed suit as we stayed low and ran up to the house. I turned the doorknob to open it slightly and Chris kicked it completely open.

POW! One of the men went down. POW! Another one went down. POW! The third one went down. I aimed at the fourth and this pussy jumped behind Alexis. There was no way in hell I was going to take the chance that I may shoot her.

"They aren't here to hurt us. Boss Lady sent a payment here," Vanessa explained, getting up from the floor. I didn't even see her over there. That's the type of shit she has to show me. Shit, I'm practically big brother now since I'm with Alexis and she about to be with Chris.

"Bullshit!" Alexis yelled with too much base in her voice. I've been trying to figure out what her problem is because she's been bitching at everyone lately, including me.

"Bitch, shut the fuck up! If they wanted us dead, we would all be dead right now but guess what? We're all here and they lost six men," Vanessa said and I must admit, she had a point. She must really love Alexis because she keeps giving her chance after chance. I can look at Vanessa and tell when she's trying not to go from 0 to 100.

The weird looking guy turned around, looking at Vanessa crazy. "Boss Lady no like this," he said.

"Boss Lady need a new approach then! She was supposed to deposit the money anyway," Vanessa said, rolling her eyes. That damn girl roll her eyes so much, I'm surprised them hoes haven't fell out yet.

"She deposit if you kill alone. You had help so you split," he said, dumping $60,000 on the coffee table. *Damn, we about to get caught stealing her hits before we even had a chance to tell her*, I thought to myself.

"You have fingers," he said, turning towards us.

"Yea," Chris said, handing him the bag he had the fingers in.

"$30,000 for you and $30,000 for you," he said to me. I've never had this much money at once in my life! Hell, I've never had this much money period. Thirty fucking thousand dollars! Do you know what I can do with that?

"What is that look for?" Vanessa asked Alexis. I looked at Alexis but she wasn't looking like nothing.

"What?" Alexis asked. She was probably just as confused as I was.

The weird looking guy and the other guy left out of the house and moved one of the vans up to the door. They came in and took all of the dead bodies out the house. After they left, Vanessa's dad pulled up. I used that as my cue to get my half of the money and go to my room. Chris followed suit, taking his half to his room.

When I got in my room, I hopped on my bed and began to count the money. About fifteen minutes into counting, Alexis' lil thick ass came strutting in my room. She sat there quietly as I finished counting the money. $30,000.

"What's been up with you?" I asked, putting the money up.

"What do you mean?" she asked, sounding like her normal self.

"This attitude you been having with everybody," I elaborated.

"I haven't had an attitude with no damn body!" she snapped, bringing the attitude back.

"What about how you pushed Frankie out your way the other day?" I asked her.

"She was in the way and didn't move when she saw me coming," she said with a slight frown on her face.

"So, that makes it ok?" I asked, as she shrugged her shoulders. "What about how you been talking to Vanessa?" I asked her. She looked away. "Hello?" I said, knocking on her forehead.

"Stop it, shit!" she said, standing her to her feet.

"You haven't even been giving me no pussy!" I said, thinking maybe that's why she has an attitude.

"You've done enough to this pussy, don't you think?" she asked, placing her hand on her wide hip.

"What's that's supposed to me?" I asked confused.

"It means I took a test," she said.

"What kind of test?" I asked confused.

"I'm pregnant Phat," Alexis said, looking me directly in my eyes.

A slow smile spread across my face. "I'm fina be a daddy yo?" I asked, jumping up and down. I ran to her and scooped her up in my arms.

**Vanessa**

I have no idea what Chris wants to holla at me about because one thing for certain and two things for sure. We aren't talking about what we did and we aren't doing it again. "Let me tell my dad what happened first," I said, standing to my feet. I met my dad at the door and walked him back to his car.

"What happened baby girl?" he asked.

"Apparently Chris and Phat killed someone on the list, and mama was sending her goons to pay them," I said, as I shook my head at the way she handled this. I can't believe she's running an entire organization doing this kind of bullshit. It had to hit her hard that she lost six of her men because of pure unadulterated fuckery. All she had to do was deposit it or just send Aurel to pay them but noooo, that was too much like right. She wanted to send eight mufuckers for little ole me. I say little ole me because I'm the only killer in the house. Alexis ain't shit and the other three are thieves.

"Baby girl, listen to me. I know you think you saw your mom but you didn't. Your mom is dead, sweetheart. I buried her a long time ago," my dad said, crushing my heart. I could literally feel my heart breaking. It felt like I was losing my mother all over again. I could feel the tears welling up behind my eyes.

"You're wrong. I know what I saw," I said, trying hard not to cry.

"Listen to me Vanessa. She's gone honey. Look," he said, handing me an envelope.

I opened and pulled out a death certificate for Karen Broughton. "This fake," I said, shaking my head as I stuffed it back in the envelope.

"There's more," he said. I opened the envelope completely and pulled out different photos. I flipped through the photos, while shaking my head.

There was one of my mother's headstone. Then, one of a man digging up her grave. Then, one of them opening her casket and I could see the bones in the casket. The last picture was the last time I officially saw my mother, the day of the funeral. She looked so beautiful in her dress and her hair was so pretty and flowing past her shoulders. I could no longer hold back the tears. I started screaming and punching my daddy.

"Why would you show me this?!" I screamed, hitting him over and over. My heart felt like it was caving in my chest as I kept seeing the images of them digging her up. "Why?!" I screamed as I dropped down to me knees. "Why would you do this to me?" I asked, looking up at him from the ground.

"Baby, you needed to know. I didn't mean to hurt you. I was trying to help," he said, trying to explain himself.

"You didn't," I said, as I felt arms being wrapped around me.

"I got her Unc," Alexis said, helping me to my feet.

I leaned against her as she led me back into the house. "I just want to lay down," I said, as Alexis walked me to my room. As soon as I opened the door, I closed it because of the scent and sight before me. When Aurel came in and got the bodies, he left some guts behind. I started crying again.

"Ssssh. It's ok," she said, leading me into Chris' room. I forgot he wanted to talk to me but right now, I'm not in the mood to talk. "I need to tell you something," Alexis said, as she pushed Chris' door open. He took one look at me and ran out of his room.

"What's up?" I asked, wiping my eyes.

"You're gonna be an auntie," she said, smiling.

"Wayne's having a baby? Who's he dating?" I asked with my face frowned up.

"No silly. Me," she said, and I jumped up and wrapped my arms around her.

"Oh my gosh, I'm so happy for you! Is that why you been so bitchy lately?" I asked because I been trying to make sure I didn't have to kill my best friend.

"I guess I have been a little moody huh?" she asked with tears streaming down her face.

"A little? Naw a lot!" I said, hugging her again.

I'm so excited but now that means I have to take care of this list and my mom faster than I thought. I can't allow her to hurt any of these people. Yes, I said my mom because I know what I saw. If she wasn't my mom, then she look and sound a helluva lot like her.

"Go take a nap. I need to talk to Chris and Phat," I said, pushing Alexis out of Chris' room.

"Ugh! We were getting along," she pouted.

*Yes, she pregnant*, I thought to myself. I pushed her into the room she shares with Phat. "Bro, lemme holla at you in Chris' room," I said and left before he could respond. "Chris!" I yelled. "C'mere," I said then turned around and went back in his room.

A few minutes later, they came dragging in the room. "Yall done crying and shit?" Phat asked, looking crazy.

"Nigga, fuck you!" I said, throwing a pillow at him.

"Man, don't come in my room throwing shit around!" Chris snapped. I rolled my eyes.

"First and foremost, congratulations dad," I said to Phat and Chris looked crazy.

"Thanks sis," Phat said.

"Ah shit, you getting old bro!" Chris said, giving him dap. I guess that's his way of saying Congratulations.

"Anyway, now that Alexis is pregnant, we have to get rid of that list faster, so we can get rid of Steve and Boss Lady. I can't have harm coming to her or the baby," I explained. They nodded their heads in agreement.

"What you want to do?" Phat asked.

"Since ya'll already killed one, I say we split the rest," I suggested.

"Yeah, that's straight," Chris said. Phat just nodded his head.

"After this, I think we should all move into our own spots. Phat and Alexis about to need room. Frankie can choose which one of us she wants to live with Chris," I said and if looks could kill, I'd be dead.

"Bitch, me and you staying together!" he snapped.

Before I knew what I was doing, I had done jumped up and punched Chris in the face. He grabbed me but Phat grabbed him and pushed him out of the room. "Call me another one!" I yelled at their backs. "I dare ya!" I screamed. He pissed me off so bad; I threw all of his clothes out of the dresser on the floor. I took the pillow cases off the pillows and threw them everywhere and completely stripped the bed. Petty? So sue me!

**Chris**

I grabbed my half of the money off the table and put it up in my room. I noticed Phat didn't come back out of his room and when I looked in, he was counting it. I'm not really thinking about counting the money right now because it ain't going nowhere. I need to spit some real shit to Vanessa though and I have a feeling she's going to be hard to get. I know you thinking I already smashed so what's left but what you don't understand is that I'm trying to purchase the cow. I got the milk and it was grade A. What I don't want is someone else to get the milk, so I have to purchase the cow. If I purchase the cow, then I can build her up, feed her, take care of her, and end up with more than just milk. I can get everything the cow has to offer. I bet you're reading this like why this nigga talking about cows and shit! Good pussy will do that to ya.

"Vanessa, lemme holla at you," I said, walking back up front to the living room. I was hoping to catch her before her dad came inside. She looked at me a bit hesitant like she was nervous about what we would talk about.

"Let me tell my dad what happened first," Vanessa said and opened the door. I saw her dad was already at the door but she stepped all the way outside and closed the door behind her.

"She'll come around," Alexis said as if she was reading my mind.

"She need to or she will hate me," I said, meaning every word. When I want something, I go after it with everything I got. She will figure it out soon enough though.

I headed back to my room and the smell coming from Vanessa's room almost made me throw up in my mouth, so I closed the door. I saw the guts and shit in her room, and she's probably never going to be able to get the smell out of there.

I laid across my bed waiting on Vanessa to come back here, so we could talk. I wasn't prepared for what I saw when Alexis brought her in my room. Her face was red and wet from crying. Her hair was all over her head and her pants were dirty. *Bitch ain't fina fight me because somebody pissed her crazy ass off*, I thought to myself before leaving my room.

"Is she ok?" Frankie asked, when I made it in the living room.

"Go see," I said, sitting next to her on the couch.

"Naw, you know she gets violent when she's mad. I'll let Alexis handle this one," she said, shaking her head. The vibration of my phone in my pocket distracted me from our conversation.

**Tiffany: Hey stranger**

**Chris: I couldv sworn da phne works both ways**

**Tiffany: so do i**

**Tiffany: wanna play?**

I sat there staring at my phone in daze trying to figure out what to do. Tiffany was basically asking me if I want a threesome, meanwhile I'm trying to get Vanessa to take me seriously. "What happened?" Frankie asked.

"Life has too many decisions," I said, shaking my head.

"Chris!" Vanessa yelled, as I was about to respond to Tiffany's text message. "C'mere!" she screamed, like I didn't know to come when she called my name. I stood up and glanced at Frankie as she shook her head at me. "I wish ya'll would stop playing already," she said, then waved her hand at me like she was dismissing me. I don't know what the hell Frankie got going on but I'll be happy when somebody figure it out.

"Ya'll done crying and shit?" Phat asked, looking crazy. I can tell my boy tired of living with all of these emotional ass women. Living under one roof with three women is nerve wrecking for real, especially when they are constantly fighting with each other! I be wanting to send their asses to their rooms but I just dip out.

"Nigga, fuck you!" Vanessa said, as she grabbed a pillow off my bed and threw it at him, pissing me off instantly.

"Man, don't come in my room throwing shit around!" I snapped at her. She rolled her eyes at me and I wanted to slap them bitches out of her head.

"First and foremost, congratulations dad," she said as she looked at Phat. I was looking crazy because I had no idea Alexis was pregnant. Or is she referring to Brittany? Phat told me about the night they jumped on Vanessa that Brittany mentioned being pregnant. I couldn't believe this nigga let that shit happen. I always fuck her with a condom and still pull out when I nut.

"Thanks sis," Phat said.

"Ah shit, you getting old bro!" I said, dapping him up. "We need to talk," I whispered in his ear, so Vanessa wouldn't hear me.

"Anyway, now that Alexis is pregnant, we have to get rid of that list faster so we can get rid of Steve and Boss Lady. I can't have harm coming to her or the baby," Vanessa said, like she's the baby's daddy.

"What you want to do?" Phat asked, in a way that let me know he's all in.

"Since ya'll already killed one, I say we split the rest," Vanessa said.

"Yeah, that's straight," I said, thinking about the money that was about to come my way. It's nine names left, so that's three people a piece. Oh yeah, we are most definitely about to be on one!

"After this, I think we should all move into our own spots. Phat and Alexis about to need room. Frankie can choose which one of us she wants to live with Chris," Vanessa said, like what we just shared ain't mean shit to her. She got me feeling like the bitch as mad as I just got.

"Bitch, me and you staying together!" I snapped, wanting to break her damn neck.

I was looking dead at her and didn't see her coming until she punched me in my face. I grabbed her by her shoulders because I was about to shake the shit out of her, but Phat grabbed me. He pushed me out the room and into the hallway. "Calm down bro," Phat said, before he let me go.

"Call me another one!" she yelled, and I turned around but Phat pushed me in the living room. "I dare ya!" she yelled, pissing me off.

I had to get away from her little retarded ass before I did or said something I would later regret.

**Chris: On my way. send me your address.**

I walked out the door with Frankie hot on my trail. "Don't Chris. It's only going to complicate things," Frankie said, running behind me.

"Complicate these nuts!" I said, as I grabbed a handful of my dick.

"Just go talk to her," she pleaded.

"Fuck her!" I snapped, as I hopped in the car and pulled off. By the time I got to the stop sign, Tiffany had texted me her address.

She was actually pretty close, only about four blocks away. When I pulled up, she was sitting outside with this funny looking chick. The way her head was shaped, it looked like her eyes were on the side of her head like a fish. I stepped out the car and they both stood up and this bitch was shaped like an upside down Dorito. "What's up?" I asked Tiffany, as I looked between the two.
"This my girl, Angie. I told her about you and she wanted to join us," she said, then licked her lips.

"All ya'll bitches on something today," I said and got back in my car and pulled off. They got me fucked if they thought my dick was going to get hard for a bitch shaped like that. I headed back to the house.

When I walked in, everyone was sitting in the living room watching TV. Well, Frankie and Phat were watching TV. Alexis was sitting on the floor and Vanessa was laying on her with her ear to her stomach. I shook my head at the sight of these people relaxing like we don't have shit to do. I grabbed the picture with the number 2 on it and its tape recorder and went to my room.

"If you're pressing play again, that means John Abrams has met his maker! Good Job Sweetheart! Now for this bitch! This light skin bright eyed beauty is Melissa Robertson! She's a whore and I want her gone in the worse way! She tried sleeping her way to the top of the Johnson Law Firm but she fucked up when she ruined my meal ticket all of those years ago! She slept with a man that was going to take care of me for the rest of my natural born life and he cut me off! Kill her Sweetie and cut her eyes out because he said that's what drew him to her. Thanks baby cakes!" Boss Lady said, then the recording ended.

"Damn, I don't know who's crazier!" I said out loud to myself.

"Out of who?" Vanessa asked from the door with a smile on her face. I swear, she's bipolar.

"What you do to my room?" I asked her, ignoring her question.

"Nothing," she said smiling.

"Man, my sheets wrinkled as fuck and the comforter crooked, so you did something while I was gone," I said with a straight face.

"Oh shut up! Who are we killing?" she asked, hopping on my bed.

"I'm killing Melissa. If you're ready to knock someone off, then go get number 3. I'll be back once I'm done," I said and stood to my feet.

"Wait, you not gonna come up with a plan?" she asked and looked crazy.

"Man, I don't have time for all of that," I said.

"Don't call me a man," she said, as she looked directly at me. This is by far the craziest female I've ever run across.

"Ok Vanessa," I said because I am not about to argue with her.

I walked out of the house and didn't realize Vanessa was following me until I tried to close the door behind myself. She caught it and closed it after she stepped outside. "What the fuck do you want Vanessa?" I asked, as calm as I could.

"I got your back. Let's go," she said and gestured in front of her. I shook my head and hopped in my car. She hopped in the passenger's seat. "So, what happened to the truck?" she asked once I pulled off.

"So, let me give you the run through," I began. She repositioned her body to face me in her seat. "So, we pulled up to the bank dude work at looking for a spot right. It took us forever to find one but it ended up being him heading home, so we followed him. Man, we ain't have no kind of plan and neither one of us know how to pick a damn lock but he left the shit open." I paused because she was laughing. The sound of her laugh made me smile.

"So, what happened?" she asked, like she couldn't wait.

"Calm down baby. So look, we walk up to the door and just went right on in. Him and his wife were inside arguing about Boss Lady following them and how they shouldn't have stolen from her. Long story short, Phat kills them and sets the house on fire. So, get this, we on our way back to ya'll when a black van pulls in front of us!" I said, hyped up just from thinking about it again.

"No shit?" Vanessa asked with her mouth wide open.

"Man, if I'm lying I'm flying," I said and Vanessa started laughing.

"So, what happened?" she asked, as she leaned her body over the middle console.

I leaned over and kissed her lips. She surprised me when she returned the gesture. Our tongues danced to their own songs. BEEEEEP!!! "Oh shit!" I said and snatched the wheel, so we could go back into our lane. I looked over at Vanessa and she was laughing with tears in her eyes.

"Man, you can't drive worth shit!" she said and sat back.

"So anyway, what happened?" she asked, without facing me.

"I backed the truck up til I could turn around. Phat leaned out the window and took the driver out but another van came. They rear ended us I don't know how many times before they crashed their van," I said to sum everything up.

When I glance over at her, she was shaking her head and staring out the window. We rode for about five minutes in silence before Vanessa started talking again. "What did you need to talk to me about?" she asked without looking at me.

"Us," I said but she didn't respond. "Listen Nessa, you know something is there. Don't run from it, embrace it. Let's see where this can go," I said and she just nodded her head.

"Funny," she said, shaking her head.

"What?" I asked confused.

"Funny how you want to see where it goes with us but you haven't stopped fucking with anyone. You gotta do more than just say it because I'm not willing to take the chance without action behind it. Get rid of them, then holla at me," she said without looking at me.

"Get rid of them for what? Are we actually gonna try? If not, I'm not doing it," I said, not really meaning what I just said. I figured I would be able to get her to be my girl before I got rid of anybody for nothing.

"Don't worry bout it then," she said and got out the car.

Luckily for her, I was parking at the Johnson Law Firm. "Where you going?" I asked, as I hopped out the car.

"See if she works here, I'll be back," she said and did a light jog across the street.

## Vanessa

That conversation with Chris on the way over to the Law Firm put me on 10! How can he seriously expect me to take him seriously when he's still fucking off? Until someone can give me a good reason to give this a shot, I'm not going to. I couldn't wait for him to slow down, so I could get as far away from him as possible. I really don't even know why I decided to tag along.

I did a light jog across the street, so I could go inside to make sure we were at the right place. I passed a group of women who all looked at me like I didn't belong. I was surprised they looked at me at all, since I'm normally ignored. "Hey Melissa! Wait up!" This brown skinned lady with a really tight and short skirt yelled, catching my attention. When a light skinned lady stopped in her tracks, I knew it was her. I watched her tell the other ladies to go ahead and she would catch up to them later.

I took off full speed back across the street with a car barely missing me. I snatched the car door open and hopped in. "Get ready," I said to Chris. "There she is!" I said as I got crunk. This is my first time ever doing a hit with someone else and I'm really excited about it. We sat in the car and watched her, and the chick that stopped her strut across the street. They hopped in a Phantom and almost hit another car pulling out of the parking spot.

We pulled out right behind them and luckily for us, they drove the speed limit. We followed them for about two hours before we ended up at some low rise condos. "I can figure out where they're going faster than you," I said and hopped out the car. I quickly crossed the street, so I could follow them inside.

"Excuse me Miss!" Chris yelled out.

"What the fuck are you doing?" I mouthed to him. He winked at me as he approached Melissa and the other woman. "You're gorgeous and I just want to know your name," he said, walking up to them.

I stood there with my arms folded across my chest. "Melissa," she said and extended her hand. He took her hand into his briefly as he looked at the other chick.

"Nice to meet you Melissa but I was speaking to her," he said, as he tilted his head towards the other chick.

"Eb. Ebony James," she stammered, then looked at the ground. He raised her head with his finger by lifting her chin, forcing her to look him in his eyes. I could feel the anger rising and had to remind myself that he's just playing with her.

"Keep your head held high like the queen you are," he said and turned around.

I stood there wondering what the point was. I wanted to run up on him and slap him in the back of the head for fucking up my plan! "Wait. What's your name?" Ebony yelled, shocking me. Melissa sucked her teeth and rolled her eyes then walked off. I walked in behind her casually, leaving Ebony and Chris outside. Melissa is the target anyway, so I don't know why he was talking to Ebony!

I was too far away from Melissa to catch her but she hopped on the elevator. "Can you catch the elevator for me please?" I asked Melissa, as I walked faster to the elevator door. This bitch didn't even try to stop it from closing. I watched her look at her phone until the doors started to close. When they got about halfway, she looked up at me and smiled. Too bad for her I was close enough to stick my hand out and stop them. "Thanks," I said, as I stood behind her in the back of the elevator.

"Oh, I'm sorry, I didn't hear you," she said, then looked down at her phone again.

We rode the slow ass elevator up to the 4th floor before she got off. I followed behind her and kept a safe distance between us.

When she got to her door, I took a deep breath waiting on her to unlock it. As soon as I heard the click, I rushed her. I slammed her head into the door and roughly shoved her inside of her home. She tried to run but six inch stilettos, plus hardwood floors, doesn't add up to a safe getaway. She twisted her ankle as she fell and immediately grabbed for it. I laughed softly to myself at the sight of this rude uppity bitch on the floor in pain. I walked slowly to her as she eased away by sliding her body across the floor. She had tears streaming down her cheeks at a rapid pace.

"What's wrong, Melissa Pooh? Did you hurt your ankle?" I asked in a baby like voice.

"I'm sorry I didn't hold the elevator for you. What do you want?" she asked in between crying.

"Aw booboo, it's not about the elevator. You hurt an associate of mine. I think you slept with her man at the Law Firm and he cut her off. Sounds familiar?" I asked, as I stepped on her ankle. She screamed out in pain but a swift kick to her chin silenced her. "Melissa. Melissa sweetie," I said, shaking her lightly but she didn't move. "Fuck! Now I have to move this bitch myself," I said out loud, shaking my head.

*I can't believe Chris got me in this unplanned mess*, I thought to myself as I began to drag Melissa's body further into her home. I dragged her body to the living room and it took all of strength I had to pull her up in the high ass chair she had. I have everything I need to do the job in my backpack out in the car. "Fuck, I can't leave her in here!" I said out loud.

"You right, you can't. Looking for this?" Chris asked and tossed my backpack to the couch. He had Ebony hanging over his shoulder.

"How you get in here?" I asked, picking my backpack up.

"Same way you got in here probably. I waited until she unlocked the door and knocked her out," he said smiling. I pulled another chair away from the counter, so he could put the other chick in it. Once he sat her down, I got the gorilla tape out of my backpack and taped both of them to their chairs.

"Why you bring her up here? I could have killed Melissa and she could have lived," I said, as I looked directly in his eyes.

He leaned closer to me. I closed my eyes and puckered my lips. This nigga kissed my forehead! When I opened my eyes, he started laughing at me. "Fuck you!" I said as I grabbed a knife out of my backpack.

"No fuck with me," he said, smiling. I gave him the side eye as he grabbed the gorilla tape and taped their mouths shut.

"So, how we going to do this?" Chris asked.

"This bitch pissed me off, not holding the elevator so before I kill her, I'm going to cut out whatever Boss lady wants," I said.

"You mad because she ain't hold the elevator?" he asked with a weird expression on his face.

"Yes! Nigga, common courtesy would have made her death quick and easy but noooo!" I said, and he laughed at me.

"Shut up and hold her head for me," I said, getting my sharpened scalpel ready. He shook his head and walked around the chair to stand behind Vanessa. He locked her chin in at the bend of his arm securely. I used one hand to open her eyelid. "Get ready babe," I said, right before I slid the scalpel around her eyeball. She woke up bucking against the tape but it was too strong for her to break free. She tried screaming but the tape muffled her screams. "Hold her tighter!" I snapped, getting aggravated because she wouldn't be still. She was going to mess me up and I could possible cut the eyeball in half. It took several minutes but I got it out in one piece. She passed out from the pain. I moved to the other eye and did the same thing. Once I finished, I couldn't believe she was still alive! I could see the rise and fall of her chest as she sat slumped over in the chair with blood dripping from her sockets. I stood back and smiled at my work until I heard soft whimpers coming from Ebony. "She's all yours," I said to Chris, as I rolled my eyes at him.

"Keep rolling your eyes and I'ma cut em out like you just did ole girl," he said, making me laugh.

I stood back as I watched Chris go through my backpack and pull out the ball and chain weapon I have on a stick. It has a wooden handle with a chain attached to it. Attached to the chain is a ball that has spikes all over it. "You fina use that?" I asked with a frown on my face.

"Yea, what's yo problem?" he asked.

"Nigga, I haven't used it yet! Let me swing first," I said, reaching out for it. Chris sighed heavily as he handed me the ball and chain.

"Move back," I said, as I stood directly in front her. She was staring at me shaking her head and crying. I really hate to do this but she just happened to be at the wrong place at the wrong time. I'm sure somebody told her to cut Melissa off, so she should have listened. I reared back as far as I could and hit her right thigh. She tried screaming out but her screams were also muffled. I yanked on the ball but the spikes were caught in the meat of leg. I yanked and yanked until it broke free. Blood and muscle tissues flew everywhere! It was indeed a sight to see.

"Man, what the fuck?!" Chris yelled, causing me to turn around and look at him. The sight was extremely funny. He had a big chunk of her thigh on his forehead and blood splattered all over his face.

"I told you to move back," I said laughing.

"That shit ain't funny," he said, snatching the ball and chain from me. He came down hard on the top of her head. When he pulled back, it hadn't gotten stuck. He walked over to the kitchen and cleaned it off before returning it to my backpack.

"You mad?" I asked because he was walking around like he had an attitude.

"Man, shut up talking to me," he said, as he grabbed a lighter and set fire to the curtains in the living room. My first instinct was to look up thinking the sprinklers would come on but they didn't have any.

"What I do?" I asked, as I watched the fire burn. "You got that shit on me! C'mon, so I can go hop in the shower!" he snapped, grabbing my arm and backpack at the same time.

By the time we left, the fire had spread across the entire living room. We took the stairs two at a time and didn't see a fire alarm until we got to the first floor. I pulled it and Chris stopped running, causing me to run into him. "What the fuck you do that for?" he asked, frowning at me.

"You have blood on you. If we walk out of here, these white folks gone be looking at you like you did it. In a few seconds, everybody gonna be running out and we can blend in," I explained. We stood at the door leading to the lobby a few seconds before the tenants started to flood the lobby from the other staircase door. Chris ran his hand down his face before he pulled me through the crowd of people, trying to make an exit.

It took us no time to get to Chris' car and we headed home.

## Phat

Since Vanessa came in our lives, things have been hectic but in a good way. If it wasn't for her, we would still be robbing people and risking our lives for chump change. It was so many times that we set out to rob a nigga and came back empty handed because we hit him at the wrong time. Shit was so stupid. Now that I have a baby on the way, I can't do that shit no more. Vanessa is right about Alexis and I needing more room because I don't want my kids spaced out too far. Now that Alexis is about to give me my possible first child, she's going to stay pregnant.

"Baby, how many kids do you want?" I asked Alexis, as we sat in the living room watching TV with Frankie. I think everybody has been worried about her but nobody has tried to figure what's wrong. She's been acting like this since she shot Alexis. I know shooting Alexis isn't the problem because Alexis forgave her, and they have been getting along just fine.

"One," Alexis said, without taking her eyes off the TV. Vanessa and Chris had just left to do the next hit but I was wishing one of them were here to back me up on this.

"I want six. Baby, can we meet somewhere?" I asked.

"Six!" Alexis and Frankie yelled simultaneously.

"Yea," I said calmly. I know six is a lot and I don't really want six, but I do want at least four.

"Naw baby, I can't do six, maybe three," Alexis said, looking at me.

"Give me four, baby," I said, sitting on the edge of the couch.

"Nigga, you should have taken three, now we only having two," she said laughing. Frankie joined in but I didn't see a damn thing funny.
"Whatever," I said, sitting back when there was a knock on the door.

I stood up and swung the door open. It was the dude from the other day that came to bring me and Chris' money. "Come in peace," he said, as I stepped to the side. He walked in and gave Frankie and Alexis a head nod but neither of them acknowledged him.

"What's your name?" I asked him.

"Aurel," he said. I nodded my head. Two men came in carrying two duffel bags a piece.

"What's all of this?" I asked Aurel.

"Payment," he said, simply taking a seat.

I stood there looking crazy, wondering how much Boss Lady paying them to kill that lady. About thirty minutes later, Chris and Vanessa came strolling through the door. Chris was mugging the fuck out of everybody that didn't belong. "What the hell? Are ya'll following us?" Vanessa asked, as she sat her backpack on the table.

"No. We follow target," Aurel said, standing to his feet.

"Well, why ya'll won't kill them?" Chris asked.

"Your job. You have eyes?" Aurel asked.

I was confused until Vanessa pulled a bag out of her backpack. "Who eyes? Ew!" Alexis asked.

"Melissa," Vanessa said, as she tossed the bag to Aurel. My stomach turned at the idea but I'm getting use to the gruesomeness that comes with Vanessa.

"You get $80,000 a piece," Aurel said, before snapping his fingers. At the snap of his fingers, all four bags were placed on the coffee table. I looked at Chris and his mouth hit the floor.

"Shit, I'm the only one without no money. Let me do a hit," Frankie said, causing everyone to laugh.

"Why so much?" Vanessa asked. I laughed when Chris pushed her.

"Shut up!" he snapped at her.

Aurel chuckled lightly before responding. "You kill two people on list," Aurel said.

"What the fuck? How ya'll knock two of them out at once?" I asked, confused. Aurel picked up a picture off the coffee table with the number 3 on it.

"Ebony James. Whore," Aurel said, showing us the picture.

"Well, look at God!" Vanessa said. "What?" she asked, as she shrugged her shoulders. Everyone was looking at her crazy after she said that. "I'm just saying," she paused to laugh. "Thank God for small favors," she continued.

I shook my head as Aurel and those guys left the house as quickly as they showed up. "So, the next one is mine," I said, grabbing the picture with a number 4 on it.

"I'm going with you. I'm going to be the only one without any money!" Frankie said, sounding like her old self.

"As long as you don't start crying," I said. Vanessa started laughing but Alexis and Frankie both gave me side eyes.

"What's the plan?" Vanessa asked.

"We're winging it," I said, as I grabbed the tape recorder and pressed play.

"Hey Sweetheart! Moving right along I see. The photo you are looking at is of Eric Smith. Eric works for the NYPD but he lives not far from you. Flip the picture over and you will see his address. He has a wife and two children. There was recently a drug bust and they collected 40 million dollars. My inside guy was going to get my money out of evidence and bring it to me but there was a problem. Eric only turned in 12 million dollars, meaning he stole the rest! I want you to hog tie him like the pig he is and shoot him in the head. I don't want the money he stole because it's the principle that matters. If you find the money, it's yours. This job will pay you $30,000 because I'm sure you're going to find the other money. Thanks!" The tape recorder ended.

I looked around the room at nothing but open mouths. Everybody's jaw was on the floor after hearing how much money Frankie and I were about to make. "Man, we ain't gone have to rob or kill people when we find that money!" Frankie said excitedly. I nodded my head because my mind drifted off to thoughts of my unborn. This money will have my kids set for life.

"Baby, did you hear her?" Alexis asked, snapping me out of my thoughts.

"Naw, what's up?" I asked, looking between Vanessa and Frankie because I didn't know who said something to me. Vanessa laughed and pointed at Frankie.

"How we gone do this?" Frankie asked.

"Let's go to the police station. You walk in and see if he's at work or not," I suggested, just to throw something in the air. Vanessa frowned but didn't say anything. She walked to the back of the house and Chris followed her.

"I wonder what they're going to do about Vanessa's room being out of order," Frankie whispered and Alexis laughed at her.
"Shit they gone sleep together, let's go Frankie," I said, grabbing the picture and a set of keys. Vanessa bought everybody a car but we hardly ever drive the one she gave us. We mostly just grab a set of keys and take whatever vehicle they go to.

"Be careful ya'll!" Alexis yelled out the door once we reached the car. I winked at her and hopped in while Frankie gave her a head nod. I drove around aimlessly, trying to figure out if this was a good move or not. It would be safer and easier to wait outside his house for him to come home. It was getting dark, so hopefully, we would blend in with the night and no one would notice us sitting idle in the car.

## Chris

Man, I couldn't wait to get home and get this shit off me. Vanessa's careless ass got that bitch's blood all over my face! It was smart of her to pull the fire alarm because I was about to get us caught! I didn't even think about anyone being able to identify me. My only concern was getting in the shower. I didn't say shit to her the whole way home.

"What the fuck done happened now?" I asked out loud to myself when I saw a black van in the yard. They had already come back for their other vans after they told us we could keep them, so I wonder what's up now. Vanessa hopped out the car and strolled casually to the door like she already knew what was happening inside. I shook my head and followed her to the door. When we walked in, there were three men standing in the living room. Two of them had two big duffel bags a piece. The third guy is the same guy from the last time they came. Either they're running low on men or learned to come in a less threatening way than last time.

As soon as I saw them standing around the living room like they belonged, I got pissed off. I can only imagine what my facial looked like. "What the hell? Are ya'll following us?" Vanessa asked. Now, when we pulled up, she seemed to be ok with them being here the way she hopped out.

"No. We follow target," the guy answered her.

"Well, why ya'll won't kill them?" I asked because if they're keeping tabs like this, then it should be way easier for them to eliminate their problem.

"Your job. You have eyes?" he said. *That's bullshit!* I thought to myself as I continued to mug them.

I watched as Vanessa grabbed her backpack and pulled the bag out that contained Melissa's eyes. I could feel my phone vibrating in my pocket but I couldn't grab it because there was blood residue on my hands. "Who eyes? Ew!" Alexis asked with a facial expression that was mixed with horror and disgust.

"You get $80,000 a piece," the guy said, and my mouth hit the floor! I didn't care about the dried blood on my skin or nothing anymore!

"Why so much?" Vanessa asked, and I pushed her to get her to shut the fuck up. She shot me a look that could kill but if they realized they made a mistake and want some money back, I'm going to kill her!

"Shut up!" I snapped at her stupid ass. Who the fuck asks someone why they're paying them so much money?

"You kill two people on list," the guy answered her. I tilted my head sideways as I looked at him with a confused expression on my face.

"What the fuck? How ya'll knock two of them out at once?" Phat asked, looking at me how I was just looking at ole boy.

The guy walked over to the table and showed us the picture of the other chick. A slow smile spread across my face because we are that much closer to getting Steve! I can't wait to hear him scream out in pain and beg for his life before I kill him. "Ebony James. Whore," the guy said.

"Well, look at God!" Vanessa said, and my mouth hit the floor. This has got to be the craziest female I've ever encountered in my life! "What?" she asked, once she realized everybody was looking at her like something's wrong with her. "I'm just saying. Thank God for small favors," she said, causing me to laugh softly to myself.

After the guy left, Phat grabbed the next picture and said he's going to kill that one. With the help of Frankie, he should be good, as long as she don't have an emotional break down... again! She's just starting to come around to how she was before she shot Alexis and I think everybody has noticed it. The only problem I see is that they're going to kill a police officer with no plan. Phat's ass said they're going to wing it! What kind of bullshit is that? If I was them, I'd plan this one carefully, so I could get the money he stole too! Man, after we finish this list, we all will be set for life!

I couldn't stand around talking to them like I didn't have blood on me so when Vanessa walked out, I followed her. "Why you be acting like a puppy?" Vanessa asked, walking down the hall.

"The fuck you mean?" I asked, getting pissed off.

"Following me like a lost puppy," she said, looking back at me. I didn't respond to her. I just walked into my room. I can show her a dog if she wants to see one. I'm not about to keep chasing this girl.

When I got in my room, I wasted no time stripping out of my clothes. Certain parts of my shirt were hard and crusty. The blood on my skin felt like sandpaper and I could smell it! The smell was starting to get to me as I made my way into my bathroom. I turned the shower water on and hopped in without adjusting the temperature. It burned like hell at first but once the smell of Dial filled the air, I didn't care. I bathed in the shower until the water turned cold. I felt like a new nigga as I walked out the bathroom with the towel that I dried off with around my waist.

Vanessa was sitting on my bed with her hair wet reading a book. "Man, get the fuck off my bed!" I yelled. My voice boomed off the walls and startled her. The expression on her face was quite amusing as it went from blank to scared to pissed, in a matter of second. I didn't laugh because it wasn't shit funny about her being in my bed with wet hair.

"You need to learn how to talk to people," she said, as she rolled her eyes and climbed off my bed. She sat in the chair that isn't too far away from the bed and continued to read. I shook my head as I walked to dresser to get some clothes out. "Oh my gosh, Chris! Go in the bathroom!" she shrieked when I removed the towel to get dressed.

"Girl, this my room! Take yo ass in yo room or something," I said, as I looked at her red cheeks. I'm naked but she's the one embarrassed. I turned completely around to face her and hit the Quan. The look on her face was priceless as I watched her jaw drop!

"I can't stand you," she said with a slight smile on her face. It's funny how she's basically pitching a fit because I'm naked, but she hasn't looked away.

"Why you didn't dry your hair off?" I asked, as I slipped into my boxers. I threw on some sweatpants and a muscle shirt before I jumped in my bed.

"My body is tired and I just wanted to lay down," she said as she looked up from her book. I looked closer to see what she was reading. When she caught me, she held it up, so I could see it clearly.

"Why are you reading that?" I asked curiously. When I first saw her with a book, I thought it was one of those urban fiction books a lot of girls read.

"When I catch up with my mom, I need to know how deep to cut to skin her alive and torture her without hitting an artery," she said, as she looked directly at me.

The plan is to start taking notes from Vanessa, so I can be there for her if she needs me. She moves fast like a cat and she's light on her feet. I know she hasn't had any training, so she must have taught herself. I guess that goes for her teaching herself about human anatomy by reading that book.

We finally got a break to relax before our next hit because Phat and Frankie are on their way to complete the fourth hit. It's getting late anyway, so we'll be able to knock the fifth hit out tomorrow. I stared at the TV until my cellphone began to ring. Vanessa looked at it then at me before she tossed it to me. I thought she was about to answer it but I don't even think she looked to see who it was.

"Yea?" I said, as I answered the phone.

"Well, hello to you too," she said.

"Man, why you on my line?" I asked because I could feel myself getting aggravated.

"Why'd you leave?" she asked in a whiny childlike voice.

"Tiffany man, what the fuck do you want?!" I snapped. Vanessa jerked her head in my direction and gave me a look I couldn't read.

"YOU!" Tiffany screamed in my ear.

"Calm down. There's no need to do all of that," Vanessa said as she reached out and placed her hand on my leg. Her touched calmed me immediately.

"Naw ma. It ain't even that type of party," I said, as I looked at Vanessa. She had started back reading her book like I wasn't in here on the phone with someone else.

"Oh, so I'm good enough to fuck and that's it?" she asked. I could only imagine how hard she was rolling either her neck or eyes. Shit, probably both.

"You offered it and I accepted it. That was it. If you wanted more, you should have done shit differently," I explained then hung the phone up.

Not even ten seconds later, it was ringing again. I glance at the caller ID to see that it was Tiffany calling back. I hit the volume button to silence the call and placed on the bed. A few seconds later, it started ringing again. I let out a deep exasperated breath and silenced the call. I closed my eyes and began to rub my temples because I could feel a headache approaching.
"Hello?" Vanessa answered the phone. I cut my eyes at her and she winked her eye in return. "This is Vanessa. You don't know me and I'm almost certain that it's not in your best interest to get to know me. All I want you to do is stop calling Chris. When I hang the phone up, if you call or text this phone again, I'm coming to your front door," she said and then hung the phone up.

We shared a quick glance before we both burst into a fit of laughter. While we were laughing, my phone started buzzing out of control. When I picked it up, Tiffany had sent me so many messages, I didn't know what to do to shut the damn phone up. I looked over at Vanessa, who had this weird smirk on her face. "Let's go," she said, standing to her feet.

**Frankie**

First off, let me start off by saying my name is not Frankie. It's Francesca Johnson. I have no idea why my mom named me that. I'll never forget her or my drill sergeant ass daddy!

*Past.... "Ann baby, here, take your medicine." my dad, Andrew, said to my mom. Every night, he would make her take medicine that would make her fall asleep. Once he made sure she was asleep, he would come put me to bed. It all started after he came back from Afghanistan. I don't know what happened to him over there but I wish that it hadn't. It was like living with two different dads.*

*In the morning, we all had to be up at 6am and eat breakfast by 7. I had to be at school by 7:45am, so I would always get dressed before breakfast. After school let out, we had to have the house spotless before he came home from work at 5pm. Dinner was always served at 6:30pm, and I got my bath at 7:30pm then went to bed by 8pm.*

*I know you're thinking "aw, he tucks her in every night how sweet," but that isn't the case. Sadly, my night consisted of weaponry training. He would constantly tell me we weren't safe and I needed to be ready. At first, he would bring a gun and tell me to remove the safety switch. Then, I had to show him where the trigger was. All of that I knew from watching TV.*

*Things didn't get bad for me until he told me to load the gun one night. He never would give me instructions, only orders. It wasn't as simple as sliding the chamber of bullets in like I thought it would be. I pushed it in but it fell right back out. My dad didn't say anything though. I watched nervously as he pulled out a pack of Newport shorts and tapped the pack against his hand. He pulled one out, stuck it between his lips, and lit it before he took a long pull from it. He lifted my pajama shirt and pressed the lit end of the cigarette firmly against my stomach with his other hand over my mouth. I screamed and squirmed but my cries for help were muffled. I whimpered softly as he looked down on me like I was nothing.*

*He tilted his head towards the gun, indicating he wanted me to try again without saying a word. I shook my head vigorously. "I don't want to," I remembered saying. He took another long drag from his cigarette before burning me again. Five tries and four burns later, I finally loaded the gun. He left without saying a word and the next morning, he was back to himself.*

*That night, he put my mom to bed then came to my room. He handed me the gun in three pieces. I grabbed the magazine first and loaded the gun, since I already knew how to do it. The other piece was the barrel of the gun that goes at the top. My hands began to tremble as I watched him pull a cigarette out of the pack. I had no idea how to put the barrel of the gun back on it. At the time, I didn't know it came off! I sat it on top of the gun and pressed down but it fell off. I watched my dad take a pull from his cigarette with a look of pure terror. He used his free hand to lift my pajama shirt and burned my stomach. I winced in pain, plus, I was still sore from the previous night.*

*I began to cry but my tears did nothing for him. He nodded towards the gun, so I picked the pieces back up. I tried sliding the barrel across the top, hoping it would click into place but it fell back off. I cried harder as he burned me again. I kept trying but I couldn't get it to snap together. Finally, after twelve failed attempts, it snapped into place. The crazy thing is how simple it would have been had my dad told me how to do it before telling me to do it. I couldn't sleep because my stomach was hurting so bad. The next morning, I threw us off schedule and got a whooping by my dad because I was moving too slow.*

*The following night, he brought me the pieces again. I couldn't concentrate due to the pain, so I messed up five times before I put it together. It took four nights of getting burned over and over before I could put the gun together without making a mistake.*

*My next form of torture came when he brought a blindfold in with him. He sat the pieces on my bed and tied the blindfold around my head. I sat as still as possible until he cleared his throat. I knew what he wanted me to do but I couldn't see anything. I grabbed a piece but I couldn't tell what piece it was. It didn't fit. I smelled cigarette smoke and began to soak the blindfold with tears. I felt him raise my pajama shirt and burn me with the cigarette. About eight tries later, I had finally put the blindfold together successfully.*

*The next two weeks were pure torture because that's how long it took me to be able take the gun apart and put it back together blindfolded with no mistakes. By this time, I had long since ran out of room on my stomach, so I had cigarette burns on my back as well. I hadn't bathed in I have no idea how long because it hurt too bad to sit in the water. I would stand next to the tub and wash under my arms and between my legs. I was only a little girl and no little girl should have been going through what I went through.*

*Once I perfected the craft of dissembling and reassembling, we moved on to my next lesson. I was so proud of myself because I had gone an entire week without getting burned or even having to smell those Newports. We started skipping dinner and he would put my mom to bed earlier than usual and take me out back for target practice. As weird as it may seem, I was actually excited about being able to actually use the gun.*

*At this time, we lived in Bogalusa, Louisiana and my dad owned 6 acres of land. The only house on the land was the house we lived in, so shooting in our backyard wouldn't disturb a single neighbor. Hell, we were the only family on the block. Anyway, when I approached my dad, I noticed he was standing next to a red line that had been spray painted on the grass. On the other side of him was a dark brown Indiana Jones style whip on the ground. I studied the yard and noticed he had cans sitting on the top of our picnic table. He handed me the gun and pointed at the picnic table. I extended my arm and aimed at the cans before I started to shoot. I emptied the clip and all 6 cans were still on the table.*

*"Turn around," my dad said to me. I turned around slowly and glanced back at him. I watched him bend over and grab the whip. My fight or flight senses kicked in and I ran away. Before I got far, I felt the whip connect with my back. I fell over onto the ground in pain. I knew I was bleeding because I could feel my shirt getting wet. He came down on my back again as I screamed out in pain. This happened daily but I eventually got so good with guns that I hardly ever got whipped again. One day, my dad came home with a machine gun and I knew my training was about to start all over. I grabbed my mom's medicine and poured them all out and my dad was so furious, he whipped me until I passed out. When I woke up, I was in the hospital and both of my parents were locked up on child abuse, child neglect, child endangerment, and attempted murder charges. Not long after that, I bounced around from home to home until I ended up at the group home with my brothers.*

"Please don't tell me bringing you along was a mistake," Phat stated. His voice snapped me out of my thoughts of the past and I whipped my head in his direction.

"What is that spose to mean?" I asked with attitude laced through my voice.

"Man, you been spaced the fuck out over an hour. I ain't said shit because I was giving you a chance to focus!" he snapped at me. His grey eyes turned a shade darker as he looked over at me.

"I'm good," I said, as I looked away. I noticed we were in a nice, quiet neighborhood. I saw a kid heading in our direction with one of those little Chihuahua dogs. When they got by our vehicle, it started barking like crazy. I watched Phat stick his arm under the seat and I took a deep breath. The little girl pulled her dog away roughly by its leash. Phat removed his arm from under his seat as I sighed a breath of relief. "Which house is his?" I asked. Phat grabbed the picture from the back seat to check the address written on the back of the photo. He looked around for a brief moment then pointed at a red brick two story home. It looked perfect in every way, from the green grass that was manicured perfectly to the white picket fence that surrounded the entire yard. There was a huge tree in front of the house with a tire swing hanging from one of the branches. I've seen those things around but I've never actually been able to swing on one. Anyway, there were two bicycles that were leaned against the side of the house, but no car was in the driveway.

"I don't think he's home," I said, stating the obvious.

"No shit?" Phat asked, like he really wanted to know.

"Let's go in and wait for him," I suggested, as I reached for the door handle. Phat's eyes got as big and as round as saucers as he watched me get out of the car. I jogged across the street, being sure to pull my hoodie so tight that it would conceal my identity. Once I made it in their yard, I looked back only to see that Phat was no longer in the car. "Fuck!" I said to myself because I had no idea what my next move would be.

I walked up to the front door like I owned the place and knocked. I know you're thinking "this bitch is stupid!" but you catch more flies with sugar than shit. "Who are you?" a little girl with long black curly hair asked after she swung the door open.

"Ashley, what did I tell you about opening my door?!" a slim dark skinned lady snapped as she rounded the corner. "Who the hell are you?" she asked with her nose turned up in disgust.

"Your worst nightmare," I stated calmly before I grabbed Ashley by the nape of her neck. "Don't scream or the kid gets it," I said, as I pulled a gun from my waistband.

Memories of that whip flashed through my mind as I gripped the cold steel. I could smell the Newport cigarettes. "Ouch! You're hurting me," Ashley whined. I squeezed her neck tighter as the smell of cigarettes grew closer. I didn't know what to do. Last time I checked, my mom and dad both had life without parole.

"Where is he?" I asked.

"Owww, Mommy, make her stop!" Ashley said as she tried to squirm away from me.

"Why are you doing this?" the mom asked with tears of her own streaming down her dark cheeks.

"If you gone knock, at least make sure you have eyes on everybody in the house," Phat said, as he rounded the corner with a little girl that looked identical to the mom draped across his shoulder.

"Put that shit out!" I snapped at Phat, who was smoking a cigarette. He looked at me crazy before putting the cigarette out against the wall and thumping the bud across the room. "Don't leave the bud stupid!" I snapped. I shook my head and smiled slightly. I was just glad that it wasn't my dad coming around the corner.

"Is she... is she dead?" the mom stuttered.

"No," Phat answered as he laid the child on the sofa. She raced to the couch, completely forgetting about the one standing next to me crying but a quick punch to the face sent her on her ass. I laughed softly to myself as Phat placed her on the couch too. "Come in and close the door," Phat said. I couldn't believe that we'd been standing in the doorway and nobody screamed for help. If there was a time to scream, that was it. I closed the door and forced Ashley into the house. I was almost lost in thought again due to the faint smell of cigarette smoke until Ashley stomped on my foot really hard. I yelled out in pain as she took off running. Phat back handed her hard as fuck and sent her flying into wall. She bounced off the wall and hit her neck on a table that probably should not have been there anyway. The impact from the fall caused her to break her neck. By the time she hit the floor, she was already dead.

I looked up at Phat, who shrugged his shoulders, before he turned his attention to the two that were unconscious on the couch. "Should we tie them up?" I asked. I'm so use to Chris being in charge and barking orders that I really don't know what to do when he's not around.

"Go find something," Phat said. I didn't respond. I simply walked through the house looking for something to tie them up with. The first room I came to was full of toys and luckily, there were jump ropes sitting on top of the toy chest. I grabbed them both and walked back into the living room to give them to Phat.

"Start looking for the money while I tie them up," Phat commanded and I felt an all too familiar feeling between my legs. There had been so many times I've wanted to have sex with Phat but didn't know how to say anything to him. I use to hear all the rumors from the girls he was sleeping with back at the group home and I just wanted to see if they were true. I stayed stuck to him and Chris like glue, hoping that one day I'd get a sample of him. It was just my luck when they started to view me as a little sister. It forced me to keep all of my feelings to myself. I gave every female Phat was screwing an extremely hard time because they were getting what I wanted from the man I wanted it from. I didn't even realize I was in love with him until Vanessa blurted it out like it was nothing. Hearing her say it forced me to consider it, and she was right.

I sighed heavily and walked up the stairs. I figured I'd check upstairs first and then look everywhere downstairs. I walked in the master bedroom and couldn't believe the bed wasn't made. Looking at the mother, she looks like someone that would keep a clean and tidy room, but this room was everything but clean and tidy. There was a dirty clothes hamper near the closet door that was overflowing with dirty clothes. I grabbed the hamper and poured everything out onto the floor. I opened the closet door and there were shoes everywhere! I kicked them around until they all ended up in one corner of the closet. I snatched all the jackets off the hangers and pulled everything off the shelf, but there was no money there. I walked to the bed and flipped the mattresses off one at a time and made sure I checked for a hole. No money. I pulled all of their clothes out the dresser and threw them on the floor and still no money. I walked out of the room feeling defeated.

Not one to give up easily, I walked into the room next door and the strong smell of piss invaded my nostrils, causing me to gag slightly. I didn't know where it was coming from until I started flipping the mattresses over and saw the huge yellow stain. I frowned and shook my head in disbelief. I made my way to the closet but it was empty, so I emptied the dresser and didn't find any money.

The next room was worse! Clothes and toys littered the floor. At first, I thought it was Ashley's room until I saw used pads under the bed. I turned my nose up the same way their mom turned her nose up at me. I flipped the mattresses over and couldn't believe how many bottles were under her bed. I didn't know what was in them until I knocked one over accidentally. I'm sure they have bathrooms and I'm sure they work. What I can't figure out is why is one of them pissing in the bed and the other pissing in bottles? I've been through a lot at the hands of my father and I've never not even once pissed on myself!

I shook my head and went into the only clean room I'd been in. The bed was made and the dresser and closet were empty. That lead me to believe that this is the guest room and the only room that's never occupied. I shook my head and walked down the stairs. I thought it was strange that there were no bathrooms upstairs but two of them downstairs. I guess that's one reason why those little girls go in their rooms.

Click! When I heard the cocking of a gun, I turned around slowly. I stood face to face with Officer Eric Smith. I immediately began to wonder where Phat was and how he got passed him without me hearing anything. "Who are you and why the fuck are you in my house, bitch?!" Officer Eric Smith asked. At this very moment, he did not sound like an officer of the law. He sounded like my worst nightmare. The grim reaper.
"You stole from the wrong woman," I said as I steadied my voice, so I wouldn't sound as scared as I was.

"You fucked with the wrong nigga!" he countered then fired a shot at me.

Luckily, I was staring at his trigger finger and ducked at the slightest movement of it. My swift movement caused the bullet to miss my head by inches as I squeezed by him and ran out the bathroom door. Pow! Pow! Pow! He fired round after round as I ducked into the first room I went in when we first got here. I fell as soon as I entered it and kicked the door closed. I hopped up and ran to the window, so I could open it and climb out. It didn't matter that he saw my face and I'd probably go to jail. All that mattered was my life at this moment.

Boom! He kicked the door open and it got stuck in the wall behind it. I jumped around to face him. I held my shaking hands as high as I could to let him know I surrender. He smiled a devious smile before he pulled the trigger. POW!

**Vanessa**

I tried going in my room and cleaning the guts up but the smell proved to be too much for my stomach. I grabbed some clothes to put on after my shower and headed to the bathroom. As I waited for the steam to fill the bathroom, I stripped down to nothing and sat on the toilet. Once the bathroom was nice and steamy, I adjusted the water temperature and stepped into the shower. The warm water felt so good beating against my naked body. I began to imagine each pellet of water being sweet kisses from Chris' mouth. I let out a low moan as my hand found its way between my legs. "What the fuck are you doing girl?" I asked myself out loud, as I removed my fingers.

I grabbed a washcloth and began to soap my body up as my thoughts traveled to the ten people we have to kill. "My damn work phone hasn't rung at all since we got the list from boss lady," I said out loud to myself. I sure as hell hope she's not messing with my money! Who am I kidding? She's paying way more than I was charging. I stood under the shower head until there were no more suds on my body. My head started to itch, so I quickly washed my hair and climbed out the shower.

I made my way back to my room to get my Human Anatomy book then went to Chris' room to study. I should have known he would flip the fuck out about me sitting on his bed with wet hair because he's always flipping out when it comes to his bed. I really don't care about his mouth anymore. I guess you can say he's growing on me. I didn't even argue with him; I just sat in the chair that's in his room and continued reading.

His phone started ringing and it was that bitch Tiffany. Jealousy filled my body instantly. That's why as soon as I got the chance to talk to her, I did! I told that bitch not to call or text him no more and you know what she did? Texted him! Bitch must not know about Vanessa Broughton! Hell, she can't know because I'm just now figuring it out!

"Let's go!" I said to Chris before I walked out of his room. I was wearing black sweatpants and a t-shirt with my hair pulled up in a wet messy bun. I didn't see Chris until I made to his car. "Man, what you trying to do?" Chris asked.

"Beat that ass," I said calmly.

"Man, I'm not taking you to her," he said, as he shook his head.

"Why because you care about her?" I asked. My body was riddled with anger as I waited on am answer I never got. Chris turned his back on me and walked back inside.

I sat in the car for five minutes waiting on him to come back outside but he didn't. "I need to kill something bad!" I said out loud to myself. I climbed out of the car and slammed the passenger's side door so hard, the window shattered upon impact.

Before I got to the front door of the house, Chris was swinging it open. "Man what the fuck you do?!" he yelled at me.

"Fuck you!" I screamed in his face before I bypassed him.

I walked straight to the coffee table and grabbed the picture with the number 5 on it and the tape recorder that corresponded to it. I sat next to a sleeping Alexis and pressed play. "Well, baby girl, you're now halfway there. The blonde hair blue eyed beauty you're looking at was my best friend, Amanda Raymond. She was the first white girl I ever trusted but she turned her back on me for a nigga! Every time I called her to vent, if he was around, she wouldn't answer the phone. One time, I was stranded and they were at the movies, and she wouldn't come get me. I want you to eliminate her by stabbing her in the back the same way she stabbed me in mines. $75,000 for her." The tape ended.

"Fuck! She didn't give me enough information!" I said out loud to myself. I got up and went to the back to get my tablet. When I came back in the living room, Chris was watching TV like he doesn't have one in his room. I quickly logged onto my Facebook account that I never used and searched for Amanda Raymond. Ten Amanda Raymond's popped up and just when I was about to give up, I found her. I clicked on her profile and the dumb bitch's profile is public, so I didn't have to send her a friend request.

I scrolled down her page and noticed how every time she went somewhere, she checked in on Facebook. I guess that's ok but not when someone's looking for you to kill you! Right now, her and the guy are at Bouley's over in New York, New York getting something to eat. "If I take the Brooklyn Bridge, I can get there in thirty minutes," I said softly to myself. I quickly googled the address and sent it to my car's navigation system, so it will pull up when I hop in. I went to my room to grab my black pullover and left.

Traffic was a little congested, so it took me forty-five minutes to get to the restaurant The big glass windows allowed me to see inside of the restaurant without having to go in. Curiosity got the best of me because I had never been inside of the building. When I walked in, it felt like home! Off to the left was a bread station. Tables were placed neatly all over the restaurant with the chairs that looked so comfortable. I bet you could eat and fall asleep at one of these tables. They had a nightstand and even a book shelf! I didn't look to see what books they had though.

I walked passed Amanda as she stood to leave and bumped right into me. "Watch it bitch!" she snapped.

"Sorry ma'am," I said with my head down. I scurried back out to my car and hopped in with my blood boiling. "Oh yeah, I'm going to enjoy this," I said out loud to myself. I watched a guy open the door for her and they walked hand in hand to his Maserati. I'll never understand what the big deal is about those expensive ugly cars!

When he pulled off into traffic, I pulled off behind them and followed them for thirty minutes until we pulled up to a brownstone. He got out and opened the door for her. I watched him walk her to the door, kiss her on the cheek, and walk back to his car. He sped off and I approached her door with caution. I had my backpack on as I knocked on the door. I waited patiently but she didn't come to the door. I turned the doorknob with my gloved hand and it was unlocked. I slipped in and closed the door behind me. I could hear the shower running, so I headed in that direction, making sure no one else was in the house. I got down low right outside of the bathroom door and pulled the biggest knife I had that could fit in my backpack before I walked in the bathroom.

"Where she get her eyes from? She get it from her mama! Where she get her thighs from? She get it from her mama!" Amanda sang and danced in the shower, doing her best impression of Juvenile. I stood there and watched her because it was extremely comical. "Fine white woman make you smile when she pass you! Damn, that girl sexy her mama got aaaaaaah!" she screamed because I snatched the shower curtain off the rod. For some reason, she tried to run up the wall! I stabbed her over and over and over in her back until she lay slumped over in the tub. I used my index finger and middle finger to check her pulse and there was none. Mission accomplished!

I stopped in the mirror and noticed blood was all over my face, so I grabbed a washcloth and scrubbed until it was light orange. I threw the washcloth in my backpack and headed home to collect my coins!

**Phat**

As fucked up as it may sound to you, this lady and her child must go. They've seen our faces and as much as I'd like to just kill Officer Eric after finding the money, I can't risk going to jail before I had a chance to spend it. The little girl was smart enough to grab the house phone and get in the closet when I found her, so I knew she would, without a doubt, remember what we look like. When I opened the closet door, I shook my head and kicked her in hers. I grabbed the cordless phone and hung it up, then pressed talk in case the call went through so when they call back, it will give them a busy signal. I probably should have gone ahead and killed her in the closet but I needed to get to Frankie.

When I made it downstairs and the little girl tried to run off, I hit her with all my might. I expected her to lose consciousness, not break her neck, but it saved me from having to kill her later. I sent Frankie on a search to find the money, so I'd have time to get rid of these bodies. I looked out the window and it was getting darker and I'm thinking Eric will be here soon. I can't afford them to be a distraction when he gets here.

I waited on Frankie to be gone for five minutes before I put my plan in motion. I grabbed the girl's dead body and carried it into the kitchen and sat her on the floor with her back against the cabinet. I placed her hands in her lap. I walked back into the living room and had to blink away tears because I'm not just some heartless nigga. I just need to make sure my child will be set for life and not have to worry about the things I had to worry about. "Gotta make this quick," I said out loud to myself as I broke the other girl's neck. I didn't want her to suffer by suffocating her. A neck break is silent and quick. I carried her body into the kitchen and sat her next to her sister.

When I returned to the living room, I heard a car pull in. When I looked out the window, I saw Officer Eric climb out of his car and make his way to the front door. I quickly grabbed his wife and slid her into the kitchen. I laid her on the floor and placed my large hands around her neck and began to squeeze. Her eyes popped open and she tried bucking me off of her but my weight over powered her. I could hear him walk up the steps without saying a word, like he knew something was off as I strangled his wife in the kitchen. She put up a good fight but it was no match for the death grip I had on her neck.

I didn't let her go until I was sure that she was dead. By this time, I could hear footsteps coming down the stairs. I knew it was Officer Eric because he's heavier than Frankie, so his footsteps are louder. I stayed in the kitchen until I heard a series of gunshots. "Fuck!" I said to myself as I walked in the direction of the gun fire. BOOM! I jumped back but that wasn't a gun shot. POW! "Fuck! Frankie!" I said to myself as I took off towards the commotion.

When I rounded the corner, Frankie was laid out in the toy room with the toy chest turned over slightly. Officer Eric still had his gun with a smoking barrel pointed at Frankie. I looked at her and she wasn't moving. I raised my gun in the air and crept up behind him and struck him as hard as I could. The blow knocked him out instantly. I looked over at Frankie again, who still lay motionless. I wanted to check for a pulse but I couldn't lose my sister and checking her pulse meant she'd be gone.

I ran in the living room and grabbed the jump rope and returned back to the room. I tied his ankles together and then his wrist behind his back before using the extra rope to tie together, just to make sure we had the hog tie right. I pulled my burner back out and shot him in the center of his forehead. Skull fragments, blood, and brain matter flew everywhere out the back of his head. I shook my head and looked at Frankie.

I threw her body over my shoulder and saw a piece of wood out of place in the large toy chest. I tried to stand it up straight but it was too heavy. I could hear sirens in the distance, so I took off running and put Frankie in the front seat and popped the trunk. I ran back inside the house and set their living room curtains on fire and grabbed the toy chest. I could barely lift it, so it proved to be easier to drag it out the house that was up in flames by the time I made it to the living room with the toy chest.

Here I am dragging a toy chest based on assumptions. Shit, it's empty but it's heavy like it's filled with something. I'm guessing it's hollowed out or something, and the money he stole is somewhere inside of it. It felt like it was taking me all of eternity to get the chest in the trunk and it wouldn't fit! I closed the trunk and dragged it to the back door on the driver's side and climbed in. I tugged and pulled with all of my might until I got it all the way in the car. I got out on the other door and saw the little girl and her dog from earlier standing across the street from me. "Fuck!" I said, shaking my head as she stared up into my face. *No witnesses*, I thought to myself before shooting her in the chest.

I hopped in the driver's seat and pulled off, just as the police were turning on the street I was on. Tears welled up in my eyes as I thought about the young lives I took. I looked over at Frankie, scared to check for a pulse. I drove like a bat out of hell until I pulled up to the house. Vanessa and I pulled up at the same time, and there were two black vans parked in the yard. I hopped out the car and when I made eye contact with Vanessa, she hopped out running.

"What's wrong Phat? What happened?" she asked with panic evident in her voice.

"Frankie," was all I could say as I shook my head. Vanessa took off to the passenger's side of the car and I couldn't watch.

"Chris! Lexi!" Vanessa yelled. A few seconds later, Alexis snatched the door open. As soon as she saw me, she ran up to me and wrapped her arms around me.

"Baby, what happened?" Alexis asked, as she looked up into my eyes. I shook my head in response.

"Fuck all that, Lexi, go get some cold water!" Vanessa snapped. I looked back at her and I could see she was talking to Frankie but I couldn't hear what she was saying. I continued to stare at them until Alexis returned with a gallon of water. "Damn bitch, I ain't need that much water. Where Chris?" Vanessa asked Alexis, as she took the gallon of water from her.

"He's not coming because those guys are in there," Alexis explained.

"Oh fuck!" Vanessa said, as she stood to her feet before she took a swig of the water.

# Chris

I sat around the house pissed the fuck off that Vanessa broke the window on my car. I couldn't even believe she thought I gave a fuck about Tiffany! Common sense should have told her that I cared enough about her not to let her do no dumb shit like kill her. I don't know why she don't do like normal bitches when they feel disrespected and just whoop the girl ass. Naw, Vanessa wants to kill them. I'll never forget the night she tried to explain the logic behind her thinking to me.

*I was bored in my room alone, so I got up to join Vanessa in hers. When I walked in, she was watching Pretty Little Liars. I remember thinking, it can't be that damn many episodes for her to watch it as much as she watches. "What's good V?" I asked as I climbed on the bed and pulled her to me.*

*"This pussy, want to taste it?" she asked without taking her eyes off the TV.*

*"Girl, don't play with me! I will eat that pussy like it's my last supper and the world fina end!" I said seriously. She laughed and moved out of my embrace.*

*"Do you know why I can't give us a chance?" she asked, as she finally tore her eyes away from the TV.*

*"Why?" I asked curiously.*

*"Because I'm not built to be someone's girlfriend. If a bitch disrespect me, I'm going to kill her," she said with a blank expression on her face. I knew she was serious and that was the crazy part.*

*"Well, I can't guarantee no one will disrespect you but I will put them in their place, so you don't have to kill them crazy ass girl," I said, as I laughed softly.*

*"Naw, they will die," she said with little to no humor in her voice.*

*"Why you won't just punch her in the face or something?" I asked with a frown etched on my face.*

*"Ha! Like I'm going to allow them to live to disrespect me again! Nigga please! If more bitches would just kill off these disrespectful bitches, the world would be a more respectful place," she said, like it made sense. I just shook my head and went back to my room.*

"Chris, why you looking like that?" Alexis asked.

"Vanessa's ass is crazy as hell man!" I said, as I shook my head.

"She wasn't always like that," Alexis said, trying to explain.

"Bullshit! Ain't no way she just got like this man," I said as I shook my head at her.

"Forreal Chris, she was a quiet, reserved killer. She was only killing animals and homeless people. I think that birthday gift took her to a new level," Alexis said as she dropped her head.

"Probably so," I said and walked to my room.

I laid down and took a nap. Just when my dream was getting good, I heard someone banging on my room door. I grabbed my gun and opened the door but Alexis was standing there looking crazy. "What you want girl?" I asked with a frown on my face. I was slick pissed off that she interrupted that dream because it was getting good and now I can't remember what was happening!

"They're back," she said, as she pointed her finger towards the front door like a lost kid.

I shook my head and stormed passed her because I already knew who she was referring to. Luckily for them, they learned from their first appearance not to try us like that again. As I peeked through the blinds, I saw two black vans and silently cursed myself for only having one gun. "Fuck it," I said to myself as I swung the door open. The guy that always brings them strolled in first like he owns this fucking place and stood off to the side. Three guys came in behind him. Two of them were holding two duffel bags and the third one only had one bag. I looked out the window again because I was trying to figure out why they needed two vans to begin with.

We all stared at each other in the living room for about twenty minutes, with no one saying a word to anyone. The three guys didn't even sit the duffel bags down. I could hear Vanessa yelling mine and Alexis' name, but I was not about to turn my back on these clowns. I don't know what they got up their sleeves or if they have something planned. All I know is as long as they're right here in this living room, then I am too.

"Go ahead Lex. I ain't leaving them in here," I said without taking my eyes off the leader. If I wasn't mistaken, he smiled at me and that pissed me off. We stood there face to face as I refused to look away from him. All of a sudden, Vanessa burst through the front door holding Frankie!

"Man, what the fuck happened?" I asked as I rushed to Vanessa's aide. I grabbed Frankie and laid her on the couch. I slapped her hard but she didn't get up. I looked at her chest and it wasn't rising and falling to let me know that she was breathing. I looked back at Vanessa as I waited on her to answer my question. She shook her head at me. She was about to tell me something when I pushed passed her and walked out the door.

Alexis had her arms around Phat as I approached them. "Move Lex," I said through clenched teeth. She stepped cautiously out the way. As soon as I was in arms reached, I hit him. He stumbled slightly but came back with a left hook that dazed me for a brief second. I shook the dizzy feeling and sent two blows to his stomach.

"Stop!" Alexis yelled, as Phat doubled over in pain. I punched him in the jaw and he fell over to the ground. The only reason I stopped is because normally Phat can give me a run for my money, but he really isn't even trying right now.

"This is your fault!" I yelled in his face before I stormed back into the house.

When I walked inside the house, Vanessa was positioned on the floor talking to Frankie in her ear. I couldn't hear what she was saying and Frankie still wasn't moving. "Man, what the fuck you doing?" I asked because I was beyond pissed off because nobody was telling me what was going on. She shot me a look that I guess was supposed to shut me up, but it only pissed me off. I watched as she lowered her head. It looked like she was crying from behind her.

"Nooo man," I said with my face balled up. "Vanessa!" I yelled but she didn't look at me. I stared at her as she grabbed the blanket from the back of the couch and spread it out over Frankie's body. My heart dropped down to the pit of my stomach as my body dropped down to my knees. Tears fell from eyes at a rapid pace but no sound was coming from me at all. I just lost my sister because of some bullshit.

I heard the door open, and Phat and Alexis walked inside the house. No one said anything to each other. I glared up at Phat, who returned the glare and still, nobody uttered a word. No words needed to be said. It seemed like forever but Vanessa had finally turned completely around. I couldn't read her facial expression, all I knew was it was void of any and all emotion.

"Why are you still here?" she directed her question at ole boy.

"We bring payment," he said but I could see the humor all over his face.

"Listen Aurel, as you can see, we lost a man today so do what you need to do and leave," she said, getting straight to the point. I heard a soft whimper and when I looked to my left, Alexis was crying softly to herself. I looked at Phat as I stood to my feet and noticed he had this faraway look in his eyes.

"I guess you get $30,000 to self," Aurel said, then looked at Frankie's body. It took everything in me not knock him off his feet.

I looked at Phat and he just nodded his head without moving. Aurel gestured for the guy holding one duffel bag to sit it down. Once he placed his bag next to the coffee table, he walked out of the house. "You do great job!" Aurel beamed as he looked at Vanessa, who stood stone faced. "You get extra. Boss Lady pay $100,000," he said, then signaled the other guys to place the bags down. Once they sat their bags down, they each walked out of the house.

I walked over to the window and watched them leave before I turned around and took a seat on the couch. I buried my head inside my hands as I thought back on all the laughs we had with Frankie.

## Boss Lady

I paced back and forth across my brand new black marble floors with silver butterflies etched in the middle of each tile. I just got it installed in my master bedroom. The tile floor in the bathroom that's in my room has the same design but the colors are switched. The tile is silver and the butterflies are black. I redecorated my room to match the color scheme of my new floors. I've been doing everything in my power to keep from stressing about this little bitch, Vanessa! I'm starting to think I'm going about this the wrong way. Maybe I should have taken a different approach. It's like she's two steps ahead of me at every corner I turn.

When I cornered them at the warehouse and she called me mom, I should have told her that I wasn't her mother. No child of mine does the shit she has been doing all of her life. Like I've said before, I only have a son. I've told no lies but I keep hiding the truth and now she's going to come for me with everything she's got. I should have killed her when I had the chance because now I think the chance is gone. Had I killed her at the warehouse, I would have saved tons of money and just got Aurel and his crew to take those people out for me.

Vanessa's killing them off in record time and I know it's because she has set her sights on something worth much more to her, me. I tried throwing her off by not letting her go out of order when it really doesn't even matter. Then I sent Aurel and his men after Chris and Phat, in hopes that they would crash and die but I ended up losing six men. Now, Aurel refuses to show up in a hostile manner, in fear that he will lose more men.

"Got good news and bad news. What first?" Aurel said, making his presence known. I didn't hear him come in but I never do, so I don't know how long he has been standing there.

"Good," I said, as I wished there wasn't any bad news at all.

"Woman down today," Aurel said. A bright smile spread across my face.
"Vanessa, Alexis, or that Frankie chick?" I asked, even though I know it wasn't Vanessa or Alexis. It's like process of elimination.

"Frankie," Aurel said. See, I knew it wasn't Vanessa because she's been on it! I knew it wasn't Alexis because then it would be two down because Vanessa would die to save her, so that leaves Frankie.

"Good! She shouldn't have joined in. What's the bad news?" I asked.

"Steve escaped," Aurel said and my jaw hit the floor!

It's impossible to escape from here, well at least I thought it was. My estate is so large; you'd have to figure out which direction to go to plan your escape; it's not something you can just do! "How?" I asked with my eyes focused on Aurel's mouth. He didn't respond; he gave me a shoulder shrug. "Kill whoever was guarding him and then find him! He's my only bargaining chip and I can't lose it!" I snapped before I waved him out of my face. I can't believe this shit and I sure as hell hope Vanessa doesn't find out I no longer have him. I know he won't be stupid enough to go to them though because they will kill him, and he knows it.

**Frankie**

"I can feel your pulse. Stay calm. Breathe slowly. I've got a plan," Vanessa whispered in my ear. I lay as still as possible as she grabbed me up and threw me over her shoulder. I was super scared but I've grown to trust her wholeheartedly. My only fear was her dropping me. I could hear everything around me and it broke my heart to allow Vanessa's plan to hurt Phat and Chris the way it did because they think I'm dead.

"I'm going to cover you up so you can breathe normally while I get rid of these fools," Vanessa whispered in my ear after Chris laid me on the couch. From the time he grabbed me until he put me down, I held my breath. Vanessa's so smart and I can't wait until I can find out her plan. I tried returning my breathing to normal but it hurt like hell. I laid as stiff as a board across the couch as I prayed silently for them to hurry up and leave because my chest was killing me.

It felt like forever but I was able to breathe a sigh of relief when I heard the door close. "Man, what the fuck happen?" I heard Chris ask.

"I was getting rid of the bodies when I heard the gunshots, man. When I got to her, it was too late," Phat answered. I felt a slight gush of cool air as Vanessa moved the blanket off of me. She looked down at me and winked before she turned her back to me. I tried to sit up but the pain was too much.

"Why you uncover her, man?" Chris asked with attitude laced through his voice.

"If ya'll would quit talking so damn much, you would know she's not dead," Vanessa said, then laughed. She stepped away from me allowing them to see and all three of their jaws rested on the floor.

"Man, what in the entire fuck! Man, that shit ain't funny!" Chris yelled, then turned around and punched a hole in the wall.

"Ok, you need to calm down," Vanessa said in an extremely calm voice.

"I need to calm down?" Chris asked with a slight frown on his face. I reached out to Vanessa but she took a step away from me and closer to him. "Yes," she said as she looked him in his eyes.

"Why the fuck would you let us think she was dead? Did ya'll know too?" Chris asked as his eyes darted between Phat and Alexis. Alexis shook her head no. "And you! Why would you just lay there?" Chris snapped at me as he took a step closer to me.

Vanessa stepped in front him and placed her hand on his chest to stop him. Tears welled up in my eyes as I watched him slap her hand away from him. She closed her eyes and took a deep breath before she opened them again. "You need to calm down," she repeated. I could see her clenching and unclenching her fist, so I know it was taking a lot out of her not to hit him at this very moment.

"Bitch, fuck you!" Chris said with spittle flying from his mouth.

We all watched Vanessa use the bottom of her shirt to wipe her face. She laughed softly before she looked back up into Chris' eyes. I couldn't see her face but I could see the anger all over his. Without warning, Vanessa reached up and chopped Chris in his throat. His hands immediately went up to his throat. She grabbed his shoulders and pulled him to her as she kneed him in his stomach. He dropped down to his knees in pain, massaging his neck with one hand and rubbing his stomach with the other one.

"You need to calm down," Vanessa said again. I think it finally got to him that he would have to hush and listen because honestly, I didn't even know what was going on. "Nobody knew Frankie was alive but me and Frankie. All Frankie knew was I had a plan and it required her not to move and she did great," Vanessa said, then turned and smiled at me. I grimaced in pain because I was still hurting so bad.

"What plan involved letting us think we lost a sister?" Phat spoke up.

"Well, the plan wouldn't have been a plan at all had ya'll not split up, now would it," Vanessa said more like a statement than a question. She was using sarcasm and from the protruding vein in Phat's forehead, I could tell he wasn't liking her at all at this moment. I glanced over at Chris, who looked like he wanted to kill her.

"Anyway! As I was saying, when I checked her pulse in the car, I told her I had a plan. I just needed her to trust me and she did. Now, I need ya'll to trust me. I know ya'll think I'm crazy and I may be but I go hard for the people I love, and it just so happens that I love ya'll," she said. I looked into the faces of everyone and saw their frowns fade slowly. "Boss Lady thinks she got us but I've figured her out. She tried to take ya'll out to slow me down," Vanessa said, as she pointed between Chris and Phat. "It didn't work. Where she fucked up at was underestimating me! She sent them here to test our power, not knowing the love in this house made us stronger. When you're willing to die for one another, it makes us all harder to kill," she explained. The way she broke it down made complete sense.

"So, what's the plan?" Alexis asked.

"Alexis, I honestly want to send you away where you won't come in harm's way but I know you ain't gone want to leave

Phat," she paused probably to let it marinate in their heads. Vanessa thinks she's slick because she knows Phat will agree. "The plan is simple. Now that we've lost Frankie, she will think we're weaker and she will back off long enough for us to figure out where she is. Now, all we have to do is get Frankie a tracking device," Vanessa said.

"Tracking device?" Chris asked.

"Yea stupid, so when she follows them back to Boss Lady, we will know where she is," Vanessa explained.
"Wait a minute now Vanessa, I don't know about this," I said, trying to sit up but it still hurt like hell. I took a deep breath and wiped the sweat from my nose and top lip.

"Ya'll really bought the whole we follow the target spill huh?" Vanessa asked. When nobody responded, she continued, "Man they follow us! Now that they think Frankie is dead, she won't be followed anymore so she can do the following."

"Frankie, don't worry," Alexis said.

"Easy for you to say," I huffed, not thinking I could do the job at all. "We will wait until after we kill everybody to go, Frankie. All I need you to do is figure out where they're going. I'm not asking you to go in alone or nothing," Vanessa said, easing my mind. I thought she was sending me on a suicide mission or something.

"Ok," I said as I sighed.

"Now, let's get this vest off of you and see how much damage that bullet did," Vanessa said with a knife in her hand.

## Vanessa

As I got down on my knees next to Frankie with the knife in my hand, I could see the nervousness in her eyes. She was breathing rapidly as I cut her pullover off, followed by her muscle shirt. "Oooh Frankie!" I said as I crinkled my nose up.

"What?" she asked, as she looked dumbfounded.

"Bitch, do you not own deodorant?" I asked with a frown on my face. I heard laughter behind me, then Frankie's face turned red from embarrassment. "It's ok, we all have our moments I guess," I said, as I stood to my feet and walked away. I returned with a soapy towel and gently scrubbed the musk away from her armpits. I positioned her arms above her head to let her under arms air dry and she winced in pain. I stared at her while silently thanking God that I gave her one of my bulletproof vests.

*Phat and Chris had just left to complete the first mission, John Abrams, and left us home alone. We sat in the living room chatting when I thought of something extremely important. A bulletproof vest. I'm not going to lie and say I never leave the house without one because sometimes I do. Hell, most of the time I forget about it but I'm fast on my feet. As I looked over at Frankie, I noticed a longing look in her eyes like she didn't belong but she wanted to. That look alone let me know that soon she would get over whatever is bothering her, and she will be ready.*

*"Frankie, lemme holla at you," I said as I stood to my feet and walked away. I walked inside my room first, grabbed my extra vest, and walked swiftly into Chris' room. A few seconds later, Frankie walked in looking five different types of nervous. I shook my head at her because you should never let a person know you're afraid of them. The way I think, I wouldn't fuck with Frankie because she's afraid of me. You guys have to know that if someone is afraid of you, they will hurt you just to keep you from hurting them.*

*"I can look in your eyes and see you want to get down with these hits," I said and her eyes lit up like fireworks on the fourth of July.*

*"I'm so ready, you don't understand!" Frankie exclaimed.*

*"I don't think you should because of these emotional breakdowns you been having and I don't understand why," I said somberly. After Frankie gave me a run through of her childhood before she got lost in the system, I had a lump the size of a baseball in my throat. I found myself swallowing over and over, trying to swallow the lump that wouldn't budge as tears sprang to my eyes. I fought tooth and nail to keep those tears at bay but when Frankie raised her shirt and turned around slowly, it was like opening the floodgates.*

*"Just make sure you wear this at all times," I said, as I wiped my face and handed her the bulletproof vest. She took her shirt completely off, leaving on only her sports bra and I helped her put the vest on. She slid her shirt back on and left out of the room.*

"Don't cut me Raven," Frankie said as a smile graced her face.

"Raven?" I asked confused. I was thinking maybe I missed part of the conversation or something while I was thinking.

"Yea. You zoned out just now like you were having a vision like That's So Raven," she explained. Her explanation was followed by laughter. When I looked back, only Alexis was laughing and that's because that was her all-time favorite show. It was pretty dumb to me but Alexis loved it!

"Fuck both of yall!" I said with a smile as I began to cut Frankie's shirt then stopped.

"What's wrong?" she asked with a frown.

"Your scars," I whispered. I watched as her eyes glazed over. I held my head down not sure of my next move.

"It's ok. They can see," Frankie said. I released a deep breath as I cut her shirt enough to rip it the rest of the way.

I unsnapped the vest and slowly removed it trying to cause as little pain as I could to Frankie. A loud gasp could be heard from behind me. I turned around and Alexis had her hand covering her mouth as fresh tears stung her cheeks. I took the time to look at Phat, who stood there with an unreadable expression on his face as he clenched his jaws tightly together. I looked over at Chris, who was staring intently at Frankie with bloodshot eyes. His already dark eyes appeared darker as all the emotion drained from his face. I turned back around to look at Frankie but she had her eyes closed tightly together.

I tried my hardest to overlook all of the burn marks that adorned her stomach as I examined her chest. The vest caught the bullet completely but the impact caused a bruise to appear the size of a golf ball. I touched it lightly and she frowned her face up but didn't say anything. "Lexi, can you get some ice please?" I asked, as I touched the area around the bruise to see if it was tender to the touch as well. It was.

A few seconds later, Alexis returned and handed me three cubes of ice. I looked down in my hand at the ice before launching it at her. "What the fuck Nessa?" she asked with a frown on her face after she stood upright again. She ducked when I threw the ice at her.

"Bitch, put the ice in a bag or something!" I snapped with a frown of my own. Alexis sucked her teeth and walked away.

"You gone let the ice melt on the floor?" Chris asked me with a frown etched across his handsome face.

"Beat ya feet nigga," I replied calmly because it is not the time for us to be at each other's throat. He walked over and picked the ice up just as Alexis returned with a Ziploc bag filled with ice. She tossed it at me aggressively and I missed because I felt a cold tingling sensation. I jumped to my feet and hit my lower back on the edge of the coffee table in the process.

"Fuck!" I said, as I rubbed my back and tried getting the ice out my pants. Hearing Frankie grunt from pain caught my attention. I looked over at her and the bag of ice that Alexis threw landed directly on top of Frankie's bruise. I shot a look at Alexis as she allowed her head to hang low.

"I'm sorry Frankie," Alexis said as she headed towards the back. "But now we're even," she threw over her shoulder. I looked over at Phat and he stormed off in the direction of Alexis.

"Mmmmh," a soft moan left my lips. I tilted my head back and allowed it to rest lightly on Chris' shoulder as he massaged my back. "Get the fuck off me!" I said, once I realized what was happening. Shit, this is all his fault hell! Had he not dropped the ice in my pants, I wouldn't have jumped up and hit my back on the coffee table. I looked up at him with a frown as he smiled down at me.

"Hey, carry Frankie in her room for me. She needs to rest and heal up before she can start tailing them," I said and looked at Frankie. The worry and pain were no longer an emotion I saw when I looked at her. It was now replaced with confidence. I smiled at her and she winked at me as Chris carried her to her room.

I grabbed my car keys off the kitchen counter and headed out the door. When I hopped in my car and pulled off, I caught a glimpse of Chris standing in the doorway. "It's none of their business where I'm going," I said out loud to myself.

I drove aimlessly until I pulled up at the brownstone I once shared with my brother and daddy. I used my key and let myself in. I didn't need to enter a code to stop the alarm from going off because it wasn't active. This was strange because my dad always activates the alarm system. I walked cautiously through the foyer and glanced in the living room but nobody was there. I heard voices towards the back of the house, so I headed in that direction.

I crept slowly along the wall, unsure of what was going down. "You gotta stop this shit Kathy! I didn't mean to hurt you but she has nothing to do with what I did!" my dad screamed. *Who the fuck is Kathy?* I thought to myself as I stayed closer to the wall.

"She's the reason you never left that bitch!" a familiar voice said. *WHAP!*

"Don't ever fix your mouth to call her out of her name again!" my dad snapped. I continued to creep alongside the wall as I made sure not to make any noises.

"Even in death, you choose her! I loved you Michael! What about our son?" the familiar voice asked. I could hear the pain in her question as her voice quivered. I shook my head as I waited on his response.

"What about him?" my dad asked cold heartedly. "You haven't even been there for him!" he continued.

By this time, I'm right outside the door that use to be my room. I glanced in and could see my father immediately standing as stiff as a board. I allowed my eyes to roam the rest of the room. Where my bed used to be now serves as a work station for my dad. He had a new computer system put in and the desk had files all over it. "I was mourning the loss of someone dear to my heart. Someone I thought would never leave or forsaken me," she said softly. My eyes danced around the room trying to find her without pushing the door completely open.

"Kathy, I'm not God," my dad said after he visibly relaxed.

"I'm going to kill her slowly and make you watch," Kathy said with malicious intent. I watched my dad cup his chest as he took a step away from her. She took a step closer and I could see the front of her heels. "You will regret the day you met me," she said through clenched teeth.

"I already have! GET OUTTA MY HOUSE!!!" my dad screamed. His voice boomed and bounced off the walls and scared the shit out of me. It must have startled her too because I could no longer see her shoes at all, so she must have jumped backwards too. "NOW!" he screamed and I could hear her scrambling to get her things. I jumped up and ran into the bathroom, so I could see her when she came out.

I watched in suspense as the door flew open with so much force, I thought it would fall off of its hinges. She walked out so fast; I didn't get a glimpse of her face. Her cries were muffled but I could still hear them nonetheless. *I have another brother*, I thought to myself as I watched my dad storm off to his room. I stayed in the bathroom about five minutes before I made my exit. I tiptoed lightly to the front door. I didn't realize I was holding my breath until I was safely in my car and was able to release it. I pulled out of my parking spot and hauled ass back home when my phone started ringing. "Thank God it didn't ring while I was inside!" I said out loud, as I pulled it from my pocket. My heart sank down in the bottom of my stomach as I watched my dad's number flash on my screen.

## Chris

I don't know what the fuck Vanessa be thinking about when she does dumb shit like what she just did. Who the fuck leaves in the middle of everything we've got going on and don't tell anyone where they're going? Vanessa, that's who. Bitch thinks she's untouchable or something but after Brittany and her friends jumped her at our last place, she should know that she's very touchable, hell kickable too. Ha! She'd kick my ass if she knew I was thinking that.

Anyway, I haven't seen her smile since her birthday, so I have an idea that will make her feel like her old stress free self again. It's dark outside, so it's the perfect time to put my plan in motion. Alexis and Phat have already gone in their room and more than likely, they won't be back out tonight. I put Frankie in her room and she took a small white pill labeled Vicodin. I had never taken it before but it was in Vanessa's bad of goodies. Before you think it, she's not a pill popper; she has everything we will ever need here in this house so we only have to go to the hospital if it's life or death.

Sooo, back to my plan. Since everyone is asleep or going in just a few, I have to act out my plan alone, which is not a bad thing at all. I grabbed my phone and called her up. The phone rang and rang and rang and just when I was about to hang up, she answered out of breath. "What the hell were you doing?" I asked as I made my way to the front of the house.

"Just waking up," she lied.

"You got comp-"

"No!" she cut me off before I could get the question all the way out.

I grabbed a set of keys and walked outside and pressed the alarm. It was to Phat's car, so I headed over to his ride. "You wanna grab a bite to eat?" I asked, as I slid inside the car.
She hesitated before responding. "Uh... yea. That's cool," she said before the line went mute. I used that time to crank the car up and turn on the seat warmer. It was an extremely chilly night out and I didn't grab a jacket. "What time are you coming?" she asked as she got back on the line.

"Now. Get ready," I said and ended the call.

I drove around aimlessly for about fifteen minutes to give her time to wash the scent of whoever had her out of breath off her. It couldn't have been a nigga like me because I'll have ya so tuned in with what I'm doing to your body that the only thing you grip is them sheets! I hit a U-turn with thoughts of Vanessa on my mind and headed to pick up my little surprise.

About ten minutes later, I pulled up and she was standing outside with the upside down Dorito shaped chick. I shook my head then climbed out of the car. Tiffany ran to me with open arms as her ugly friend looked at me with the "I just ate ass face" Kevin Hart was talking about. I ignored her and welcomed Tiffany's small body in my arms. She fit perfectly. I looked down at her as she looked at me with a glow that screamed, "I JUST HAD THE BEST NUT EVER!"

"Are you ready baby girl?" I asked her. She glanced back at her friend, then looked up at me with pleading eyes. I nodded my head then walked her over to the passenger side door as she jumped slightly from the excitement. I don't know what it is about her and this ugly ass chick she done latched on to, but I do know one thing. You have to be mindful of the things your friends do and say because when the shit hit the fan, it may just splatter on you.

I opened the door for Tiffany and allowed her to settle down on the warm seats, then closed her door. I watched closely as her friend walked slowly to me with a face only a mother could love.

Once she was within arm's reach, I opened the backdoor and helped her inside. "You look beautiful," I said to her. She smiled a big smile, showing all 47 teeth in her mouth. Don't correct me, this bitch has teeth behind teeth. She has teeth in protective custody. She has teeth on teeth on teeth.

I looked away once I felt vomit rising up my throat. I patted her leg softly before I closed the door and hopped in the driver's seat and pulled off. "So, how about we go to the new bar they just opened since they have food there too," I suggested, then glanced over at Tiffany. She smiled bashfully as she shied away from my gaze. I looked in the rearview mirror at Boo and she nodded her head in agreement, so I adjusted the mirror and headed in that direction.

When we pulled up to the bar, the parking lot was full. I had to circle the block and park at a dollar store up the street that closed a few hours ago. I sent a quick prayer up that the car didn't get towed before I returned. I grabbed Tiffany's hand as we made our way to the building. I heard Boo suck her teeth and chuckled lightly to myself at how loud it was. I guess when you have as many teeth as she does, it echoes off other teeth or something.

As we walked in the bar, I noticed something immediately. It was a Mexican bar. "Fuck!" I said to myself because they were about to get us fucked up. Mexicans can drink their asses off and the last time I drank with one, I was so drunk that I thought I was going to pass out but he gave me a shot of something else that picked me right back up. I never wanted to pass out drunk so bad in my life!

We strolled right up to the bar and looked at the menu that was in Spanish. There were only three of them that were in English, so I was sticking to them. I looked over the food and wrote my order down and slid it to the waitress. "Keep it coming," I said, referring to my drink of choice. I smiled at Tiffany and winked at her ugly friend. I can't seem to recall her name right now. Tiffany ordered wings and a drink called the fire blast. Her friend ordered a shot of Tequila and a quesadilla. We sat around talking about nothing in particular as we sipped from our glasses. For some reason, these shot glasses were tall as fuck and filled to the rim.

About halfway through their meals, they were damn near too drunk to stay in their seats. I smirked at them as I continued to eat my steak and potatoes and sip on my water. Once I was done eating, I paid our tab and left. Tiffany and her friend held each other up as they stumbled drunkenly behind me. They were too drunk to realize I was no longer slurring my words and leaning slightly. Had they been paying attention they would have noticed that since I had drunk three "shots" before they finished one, I should have been way drunker than I let on.

I opened the door for them and waited impatiently for them to get in. I found myself rolling my eyes in the back of my head like a bitch. Thoughts of Vanessa and the smile that will grace her face once she sees my surprise crossed my mind. I smiled, while absent mindedly looking at Tiffany. She looked up at me in her drunken stupor and smiled back, not knowing her fate. I strapped her in and closed her door before I proceeded to the back to help her friend. She was already out like a light and she looked way better with her mouth and eyes closed. She laid with her head to the side as I reached over her to buckle her up.

I hopped in the car and drove off towards the old warehouse we use to frequent back in the day. I glanced over at Tiffany and her head swayed from side to side. We drove in silence until I pulled up to the building. I hopped out and walked cautiously through the door as I checked my surroundings. I used my phone as a light once I made it inside. We always left our supplies here back in the day and now I need them back.

The flickering of a lighter caught my attention and caused me to halt my movements. I stared at the fire so hard until I could see two beady eyes behind it. I watched the smoker sit a spoon on top of the lighter before I walked away and continued on my search. When I made it to the back of the warehouse, I was pretty shocked to see everything still in place. I didn't want to stay inside a second longer than I needed to, so I grabbed the bag and high tailed it out of the warehouse.

When I got back to the car, both ladies were knocked out! The ugly duckling in the back was snoring loudly and Tiffany had slob leaking from her mouth onto her shoulder where it dried. The sight completely disgusted me.

I hopped on the highway and headed to the warehouse we used to house Ms. Jackson. We all have a key to it. As I pulled into the parking lot, my phone started to vibrate in my pocket. When I hopped out, it was Vanessa. "Yea?" I answered after I slid my finger across the screen.

"Where are you?" she asked. It sounded like she was walking, so she must have just gotten back home.

"What's up?" I countered, instead of answering her question. I didn't want to lie to her but I couldn't spoil her surprise.

"I'm ready," she said softly into her phone. I felt my heart beat hard in my chest.

"You know I've been waiting on you baby," I said, as I grabbed the bag out the back seat. "Stop smiling so hard," I said, causing her to laugh. I didn't know if she was smiling or not but judging by the laugh, I guess I guessed right. "Tomorrow we are going on our first date and will end it with a bang," I said, as I thought of the set up I was about to create for her.

"Ok, I'll see you when you get here," she said, then hung the phone up.

I don't know what happened while she was out but I'm glad it did. I grabbed Tiffany out of the car and threw her over my shoulder as I carried her inside. I walked through the dark all the way into the room we had Ms. Jackson in. I laid her across the table and strapped her down. She was still out cold but that didn't mean I shouldn't gag her. I went through our old bag until I found a strap with the ball attached to it. I gently pinched Tiffany's nose until she opened her mouth before I place the ball inside. I then lift her head slightly to buckle the strap down. I checked the straps to make sure she wouldn't be able to break loose before I walked over to the dismantled table and put it together. I made sure the straps wouldn't fall off before I headed back out to the car.

When I got outside, the ugly duckling had awakened and was out the car stumbling in circles. "Baby!" I called out, getting her attention. She looked in my direction and showed me all of her teeth before vomit flew out of her mouth. I turned away to keep from throwing up at the sight before me. When I no longer heard her heaving, trying to throw up, I turned back around to face her.

"Come in here, let me clean you up sexy," I said as I looked directly at her. I hoped like hell my facial expression didn't betray me because at this very moment, I'm disgusted. She looked up and smiled at me before stumbling in my direction. I stepped to the side, so she could lead the way. That way if she fell, she wouldn't be able to grab on to me. I directed her all the way to the room where I had Tiffany tied down.

"What the fuck?" the ugly duckling said out loud. She turned around and tried to run but was met with a fist to her face. I made sure to aim at her forehead, so her teeth wouldn't cut me the fuck up. The blow knocked her out immediately. I scooped her smelly body up and carried her to the other table and strapped her down then gagged her. I quickly checked all of the straps on both tables to make sure they wouldn't be able to escape before I returned.

I walked out of the room and locked the door behind me and proceeded to leave the building, and I locked the outside door as well. I hopped in my car and drove off but I couldn't help but feel as if I was being watched. As I drove home, I kept checking my rearview mirror but nobody was there. The city streets weren't buzzing at all so traffic was at it's all time low. I continued to drive and make unnecessary turns in case someone was following me until I made it home. When I pulled up, Vanessa opened the door and stood in the doorway.

## Vanessa

I drove home like a bat out of hell and didn't answer the phone for my dad until I pulled in our yard. "Hello?" I answered, after I shut the engine off.

"I've been calling you," he said in a weird tone. It was almost like a threatening tone.

"I was driving," I said, then slapped my hand over my mouth but it was too late.

"Where you been?" he asked suspiciously. I don't know if I'm reading his tone wrong because of what I heard or if he really knows I was listening in on a conversation I wasn't supposed to know anything about.

"Why haven't I heard from you?" I asked in a way, hoping I could change the subject from the direction it was going.

"I've been handling business," he answered in a softer tone. He almost sounded like my normal dad again.

"I miss you. After all of this is over, we're going to spend more time together," I said, as I made my way to the door.

"Yea, just don't get yourself killed in the process," he said. The way he said it sent chills up my spine. "I'd hate to see something happen to you," he continued. The words of Kathy began to replay in my mind *I'm going to kill her slowly and make you watch.* "Nessie, are you there?" he asked, calling me one of the nicknames that only my mom use to call me.

"Y-y-yes sir," I said, as I tried to think of something else to stop the lump from forming in my throat.

"Are you ok? I'm sorry," he said once he realized what he had done.

"I gotta go dad," I said, then hung the phone up.

I proceeded to walk inside the house and everything was quiet. To a lot of people, silence is welcoming but to me, it's loud, unwanted, hurtful, and deadly. It seems like when there's silence, your thoughts scream louder, like they're making sure you hear them. They have to make sure you follow every instruction down to the T. Memories flood your mind with vivid pictures and there's nothing to distract you from those thoughts and memories. Silence isn't welcomed around me. I don't want to get lost in my thoughts about whether or not my mom is still dead or alive and trying to kill me. I don't want to try and put together who Kathy could be because I've never even met a Kathy before. I don't want to try and figure out where or who my brother is or wonder why my dad always kept him a secret from us. I don't want to think that my dad is the reason this lady wants to kill me and make him watch.

For once in my life, I just want to be loved and wanted. That reason and that reason alone is why I picked up the phone and called Chris to let him know I'm ready. That reason alone is more than enough though. Since my birthday, everything has been moving so fast and I haven't been living at all. Time flies when you're killing people and I just want to take a break from it all and move far away and buy an island, so we can live near each other.

After I got off the phone with Chris, I began to clean up but not before allowing Pandora to play softly. I connected my ear piece but didn't put them in my ears. With everything that's going on, I can't chance being blindsided simply because I had earbuds in.

I started in the living room. I cleaned the coffee table off and stacked the pictures on top of each other in the box they came in, along with the tape recorders. It feels good to be halfway through the list because it means we're that much closer to getting the people that deserves to be got! I roamed all over the living room, cleaning and dusting, then I sprayed all of the furniture down with Lysol. Next, I moved into the kitchen and tackled the dishes, sanitized the cabinets, and mopped the floor. I grabbed the vacuum cleaner and did the hallway but I began to dread the next thing on my to-clean list.

My bedroom. I grabbed the mint spray out of the bathroom and sprayed it on the back of my hands. I used my finger to rub the strong scented spray right underneath my nose. I grabbed all of the cleaning supplies I could carry and walked into my room. I slid my gloves on and threw the clunks of guts that were left in a bag. It was fairly easy because it had hardened over the course of days.

I walked swiftly out of my room and grabbed the other mop bucket and filled it with cold water. After I sat it in my room, I ran back out and grabbed the peroxide out of the bathroom. I didn't know how true it was that peroxide is awesome for cleaning up blood, but I was about to figure it out. I poured the cold water over the blood stains and let it sit a few seconds then poured the peroxide on it. I ran in the kitchen and grabbed some salt and poured it over the foam and added a little more cold water. It looked like foam and cream once I mixed everything together over the stain. I used my gloved hands to massage the carpet and thank God the only thing I smelled was mint and peroxide. I let it sit then used cold water to clean it all up. A good bit of the blood was gone and I could no longer smell it but the carpet still had an orange tint to it.

I stood up and put away all of the supplies except for the Hawaiian Love My Carpet, carpet cleaner. I sprinkled it all over my room then vacuumed it out, and my room smelled amazing! When I walked in the bathroom to clean it, I noticed Alexis had beat me to it. She has a thing about cleaning bathrooms so she cleans them all, all of the time. I vacuumed Chris' room floor but it didn't need it because he's by far the cleanest man I've ever known.

After I ran out of things to clean, I ran me a hot bubble bath. I hadn't had a bubble bath in years. I slid my slender body in the tub and didn't realize my body was sore until it started aching, then all of the aches went away. I bathed myself and climbed out of the tub. I grabbed a t-shirt out of Chris' room and pulled it over my head. I heard a car pull up and took off in a full sprint towards the front of the house. When I looked out of the window and saw it was Chris, my heart smiled.

I swung the door open and tried striking a sexy pose but it made me feel awkward, so I stood up straight as I waited for him to come to me. He had the sexiest walk I had ever seen on a man as I watched him swag his way up to me. "Why you looking like that?" he asked because of the frown on my face.

"Why you smell like that?" I asked, as I took a step away from him with my finger under my nose.

"Bitch threw up on me," he said, like it was nothing, as he brushed passed me more than likely heading to take a shower.

I was hot on his trail as he walked in his room. "What bitch?" I asked, as I poked him in the back. "You know what, fuck it!" I said, as I threw my hands up and left out of the room. I was so ready to give my all to him but he's unable to give me his all to replace what I've given him. I walked in my room and threw myself on the bed and forced myself to fall asleep.

I don't know how long I was in my bed before I heard my room door open. I didn't turn to look because I already knew who it was. I figured Chris wouldn't leave me alone after what I said to him over the phone. I laid perfectly still in my bed as I waited for Chris to make his presence known.

"How much did you hear?" my dad asked, startling me. I jumped up and turned around to face him. I glanced at the clock on my dresser and it said 2a.m., so he should be at home sleep or somewhere patrolling or something. I hadn't heard anything about any cases he's been working on but then again, I hadn't heard much from him.

I took a minute to take him in completely before responding. He was wearing a white wrinkled t-shirt and denim jeans. When I looked at his face, I noticed he had started letting his hair grow or haven't had time to shave. His hair had grown out on his head and had he not had good hair, he'd be in dire need of a haircut. I took complete notice of his disheveled appearance because the man before me isn't the father I know. This man, I don't know who this man is.

"Are you going to stare at me all night or answer my question?" he asked, as he leaned forward in the chair that Chris positioned next to my bed.

"I don't understand the question," I lied with a straight face. He and I both know exactly what he's referring to, but I haven't had time to figure out if my beloved father is a friend or a foe.

"You came to the house earlier today," he paused as if he's trying to remember correctly. "I had company. How much did you hear?" he continued, as he looked directly into my eyes.

"Daddy, I didn't come by today," I said, giving him a confused look.

A noise at the door interrupted our conversation and I'd never been happier to see Chris than I was at this moment. "Hey Michael. What are you doing here?" Chris asked, then glanced at the clock on my nightstand.

"I came to uh… spend time with my daughter," my dad said, as he glanced away from Chris' intense stare.

"After 2 o'clock in the morning?" Chris asked and took a step closer to me.

From the tension that immediately filled the room, I know my dad is not a friend. "Yea, well ya'll been so busy during the day, I haven't been able to catch her," my dad explained.

"Yea, we had a long day today. She and I kicked it real hard. Took a break from the bull and decided to enjoy ourselves a bit," Chris said and continued his stride to me. I yawned real big then smiled up at Chris with nothing but love and admiration for him. "Oh!" was all my dad said. When I looked at him, he had visibly relaxed and I could feel the atmosphere shift.

I watched his movements intensely, being as though he's a cop. He rubbed his hands together and used the arms of the chairs to get up. "Well, sorry for waking you baby girl. Thought I saw you but I guess not," he said, as he stole a glance at Chris. I got out of bed and walked him to the door. I stood in the doorway with my heart pounding in my chest as I watched him drive away.

**Chris**

"Calm down baby. I'm not gonna let nothing happen to you," I said, as I slid my arms around Vanessa's small frame. She sighed heavily as she relaxed against my embrace. I can't believe all of the bullshit she's having to endure at once. I know not knowing whether or not her mom is dead or alive and trying to kill her is eating her up inside. I still stand strong on believing her mom is dead, by the way. I don't know who this lady is but I don't think it's her mom. Anyway, on top of that, her dad is on some crazy shit too. Shit, she's better off being with us than her family. Fuck that; we are family.

I pulled her away from the door and she took off running to her room. I closed the door and locked it before I followed her. When I walked in, she was sliding her hands all over the wall looking crazy as hell. "What the hell you doing?" I asked confused. She looked up at me and placed her index finger to her mouth to tell me to be quiet.

"I wonder what was up with my dad. He thought he saw me; that's weird right?" she asked and winked at me.

"Yea, I wonder who it was that he saw," I said, playing along.

"I don't know but we have to figure it out. I hope he isn't going crazy over there alone since Wayne moved out," she said.

"Me too. Let's go to bed," I said and walked into my room.

A few minutes later, Vanessa came in the room shaking her head. She had her notebook and pen in her hand, and she was writing in it as she walked. When she got done, she handed me the paper.

*My dad's in on it. Got another brother. Listening device in my room. Who is Kathy? She was there today.*

I read the note and my jaw hit the floor. I grabbed her and pulled her to me in the bed. I laid with her until she fell asleep, then I followed suit.

*****

The next morning, I woke up smelling breakfast. It's been forever since I've eaten an actual breakfast. I reached over to wake Vanessa up but she was already out of the bed. I climbed out of bed and brushed my teeth before I headed into the kitchen. "It's alive!" Vanessa said with a face filled with horror. Phat chuckled and a small smile spread across her face.

"What yall cooking?" I asked. Vanessa, Alexis, and Frankie were in the kitchen whipping something up that smelled delicious.

"You'll see," Alexis said, right when Frankie was about to tell me. About fifteen minutes later, breakfast was served. We ate grits, eggs, bacon, and pancakes with orange juice on the side.

"We gotta get to work," I said to Phat after we finished eating.

"I put them back in the box," Vanessa said, as she pointed to the box in the corner of the living room. I grabbed the picture with a number 6 on it and the tape recorder to go along with it out of the box before I returned to my seat on the couch. I waited until everyone was situated and quiet before I pressed play.

"Donna Walters is as close to being a goddess as anyone could get. Well, that's what I thought before I found out she's a liar and a fraud! She's a great pretender and that's all she does! She's a fame leach and will hang around whoever is currently popping. Figure out what lesbian female is currently popping and you will find her. Make it quick. $90,000." The recording ended.

"Ooooh, she must still care about this lady," Vanessa said. I shook my head in agreeance because so far, she's been asking for a piece of them but this time she simply wanted her dead. "I'm going with ya'll because I want to try this idea out," Vanessa said, then left the living room. I glanced over at Phat and he shrugged his shoulders at me.

"Aye man, when I used your car, I saw a damn toy chest in the backseat. I had a surprise to put in it but nobody mentioned. What's in it?" I asked Phat, once I remembered the toy chest.

He jumped up, grabbed his keys, and ran out the door. I followed suit. "Aye, help me with this," Phat said, as he began to pull the chest out of his backseat. Once he got it all the way out, I helped him carry it inside and to his bedroom. I stood there and watched him open it but nothing was in it. He started knocking on it like someone was going to answer him or something. I watched him with a confused expression on my face until he began pulling pieces of wood out of the box.

His face lit up and I couldn't believe my eyes when I peered inside. There was stacks of money bundled neatly together and wrapped in saran wrap. Phat pulled each bundle of money out and sat them on the floor. I shook my head in disbelief as I watched. "You gone help me count?" Phat asked, once he was done unloading the chest. I sat down on the other side of him, just as he was handing me pen and paper. *I must be the only one without pen and paper here,* I thought to myself because it seems like everybody had it handy but me.

I took the money and began counting. Every time I had to stop, I would write the amount down that I stopped at. I was grateful for Alexis when she walked in the room and started to help us count. It took damn near three hours for us to count the money. 28 million dollars. Never in my life had I been inside a house that had as much money in it as we have in this house. We all are going to be straight for the rest of our lives and what's in the house doesn't include what Vanessa has in her bank account.

"Fuck, I need a nap," I said, as I stood to my feet to stretch. I started getting this feeling that I was being watched. I looked all over the room, and Phat and Alexis ain't have their asses on me. I walked over to the window and thought I saw someone jump behind the trashcan. I took off out the house and ran around back to catch the assailant but nobody was there. "Man what the fuck!" I said out loud. When I turned around, Phat was behind me, looking confused.

"What happened?" he asked.

"Man, I thought I saw someone looking in," I said as I shook my head and walked back towards the house.

I don't know what the fuck is going on but after that bitch in the cab was following us, I know better than to ignore these feelings. I walked straight to Vanessa's room to tell her what's been going on. "Got good news!" she beamed when she saw me walk in.

"Oh yea?" I asked curious.

"Remy Bleu!" she said filled with joy that left me confused. She turned her laptop towards me and showed me one of the most beautiful women I've ever seen in my life. She put me in the mindset of Christina Milian but with hazel eyes. Her hair was cut really short but you could still tell it was curly. She was sporting a silver sparkly dress that hugged every curve on her body and flared out at the bottom. Damn *I think I fell in love with a mermaid*, I thought to myself as I stared at the picture.

Vanessa's laugh brought my attention back to her. "Stop drooling and look at the lady next to her baby," she said with a smile. I didn't even notice anyone else in the picture. I glanced at the other lady who was also beautiful but her beauty didn't compare to Remy Bleu! If Boss Lady thinks this chick is a goddess, she must have never seen Remy Bleu! The lady next to her, Donna Walters, is about as skinny as the twin Mary Kate. She's extremely skinny and dark skinned. When I say dark skinned, I don't mean brown skin; I mean black as fuck! Her black is beautiful though and her confidence makes her even more beautiful. Still, it doesn't compare to Remy Bleu. Anyway, Donna has long jet black hair that's only one shade darker than her skin tone which, is weird.

"There's more," Vanessa said, as she grinned from ear to ear. I smiled at her before I took a seat in the chair by her bed. "They're going to be at the lounge downtown tonight! Eeek!" she screamed like a fan.

"What that mean?" I asked, as I leaned back against the chair.

"We're going out tonight," she said as she got up and did the Shmoney dance in her bed. I shook my head at her. "Shit! I gotta go shopping!" she said as she leaped out of the bed.

I shook my head as she hauled ass out of the room.

**Vanessa**

I couldn't believe my luck when I found Donna Walters so quickly on my laptop. Her urge to be around famous people is what made it so easy to find her. I googled her and images of her popped up from all these people she's been dating with money, then I saw the most recent picture on TMZ with her and Remy Bleu. The article was about Remy Bleu's modeling career but it listed her new boo, Donna Walters. I googled Remy Bleu to get her Instagram information and that's when I found out where she will be tonight. Undoubtedly with Donna Walters.

I've never ever been out to this kind of party, so I need Alexis to help me shop. I ran out of my room in search of her. I ran in her room and Phat was taking something apart. I didn't even ask because I'm on a mission. "Leeexxxxiiii!!!" I sang cheerfully as I ran down the hall.

"What?" she asked as she stuffed her face with ranch flavored Ruffles. I shook my head at her and thought of the baby growing inside of her. She scheduled a doctor's appointment but it isn't until Monday morning.

"We gotta go shopping so we can go to the lounge tonight!" I said smiling.

"I wanna go," Frankie said. I shot her a look that they should all know means shut the fuck up!

"Bitch, you're dead, remember?" I asked, while doing the hand signal that says duh! She slumped back down on the couch like her world as she knew it would crumble if she couldn't go with us. I ignored her pouting as I stared at Alexis with pleading eyes. She rolled her eyes and stood up.

"Let me get dressed," she said, as she headed to her room.

"Once this is over you can come back from the dead," I said as I walked off like a zombie from The Walking Dead. I laughed at her when I heard her suck her teeth. I walked back into my room to throw my boots on.

"Vanessa," Chris said. I looked at him with curiosity all over my face because of his tone. "Baby, do you realize you're going to a mall?" he asked with a slight frown on his face.

"Yea. What you mean?" I asked, clearly confused. He smirked at me then pointed at my boots. I cracked up with laughter as I looked down at my Ashiko boots. I can only imagine the faces of the people at the mall had I walked in wearing boots made to climb walls. I slipped the one that I had on back off and carried them to my closet. I grabbed regular thong sandals. If I didn't have it so cold in the house, we would know what it felt like outside. I mean it's cold at night time but right now, I'm sure it's not that cold, being that summer is approaching fast.

I rolled my eyes at him and headed to the living room to wait for Alexis, but she was already ready. She was wearing black skinny jeans and a black and white long flowing Marilyn Monroe shirt. The only thing on the shirt in color was her lips, which were red. She had her hair pulled back in a tight ponytail with large hoop earrings in her ears. She wore red lipstick and red sandals. Her simple look made me feel self-conscious as I looked down at my own attire. I had on black thong sandals. My toenail polish was none existent and my pants had a hole in them and not the kind that's done on purpose. I had on a plain white muscle shirt that's for boys and my hair was in a messy bun. I had on no accessories or makeup. Standing in the room with Alexis right now makes me feel like a bum!

"We're gonna get you more stuff than just something to wear tonight," Alexis said when she noticed how I was looking at myself. My old insecure feelings began to come back as I subconsciously bit my bottom lip as I tugged on my muscle shirt. This is why nobody ever looks at me for more than a second. I'm standing here dressed like a freaking boy!

"You're beautiful sis, hold your head up," Phat said, then patted me on the back. Kathy's words began to play back in my mind. *What about our son?*

I walked out of the door with thoughts of my dad and Kathy's conversation weighing heavily on my mind. I headed towards Alexis' truck that she doesn't let anyone drive, not even Phat! Everybody leaves their keys on the counter in the kitchen and most of the time, we simply grab a set and drive off. Everybody but Alexis that is! She keeps her truck keys in her possession at all times. She has a 2008 all black Nissan Armada Truck with the extended end. She got to choose what she wanted because she went with me to buy everyone else's vehicles.

"Are you ok?" she asked, once we were situated in her truck.

"Naw, I need to run some stuff down to you," I said, as I buckled my seatbelt. She doesn't let anyone drive because she doesn't trust anyone's driving but her own. The crazy thing is she can't drive worth shit! Then you can't even tell her how bad her driving is because she's one of those "But did you die?" friends. You know the type.

"What's up?" she asked, as she pulled out into traffic and cut two cars off at the same time. They blew their horns like crazy as I clenched my chest. "Don't start," she said after I glanced over at her. I shook my head and gave her a run through of what happened from the time I walked in the house until my dad came to visit at 2 a.m. to get information. When I looked at her, her eyes had tears in them and she was trying her hardest to blink them away.

"Listen, when this is over, I think we should like buy an island or some shit," I said and Alexis laughed. "Forreal, we have more than enough money to do it and have our own houses on it," I continued. She frowned a bit, like she was thinking then she glanced at me with a huge smile on her face.

"Let's do it!!!" she screamed as the truck jerked.

"Yea, so um, no more talking until we're parked," I said as she laughed. I turned the radio on, so she knows I'm serious.

*****

When we got to King Plaza mall, we tore through all of the clothing stores, buying everything cute that was in my size. We had to make five trips to the truck to put my bags down and return to the store. We were there well over five hours and I was beyond tired and from the look on Alexis' face, she was too. We walked out of the mall, hopefully making our last trip to the truck for the evening. We didn't look for anything in particular for tonight but I'm sure out of $67,000 worth of clothes and shoes, I will be able to find something to wear.

"Let's go to the food court," Alexis suggested.

"Ok because that Chinese food was smelling so good," I said, as we loaded the last of our bags in the truck. The only available seats left in her truck were the ones we will be occupying when we leave here. We headed back into the mall and went directly to the food court. I think both of us were starving because we didn't say anything the entire time we ate.

Alexis threw her plate in the trash and when I tossed mines, I accidentally bumped into someone. "I'm sorry," I said without looking up.

"Bum ass bitch!" I heard her say and it stopped me in my tracks. I looked down at my attire and could feel those feelings coming back of being ugly, unloved, and unwanted as her friends laughed at her statement. I looked back at them all dressed to impress and it made me feel lower. "She's about to cry," the leader said in a whiny, childlike voice.

My blood began to boil. I began to fidget with the bottom of my muscle shirt. Alexis must have noticed I wasn't with her because she stopped and turned around. Her mouth was wide open but I had no idea why. Well, at least not until I felt the contents from the trashcan being poured all over me. I stood there frozen as the food slid out of some of the containers and dropped on the floor around me. Tears clouded my vision and not because I'm scared but because these bitches must die, and I can't kill them. I looked around at the spectators in the mall as they whispered amongst themselves.

Alexis rushed to me as she shot daggers at the girls. "Stay calm Nessa," she said, as she began to knock some of the trash off of me. I shook my head no as I took a step away from her. "Nessa, please no," she said with worry all over her face.

"Go home," I said as calm as I could, given my current situation. She shook her head no. "Well, sit down," I said as I turned around to face the three girls that stood before me.

They were recording me on their cellphones as I approached them slowly. "Ew, what da fuck ya doin, mutt?" the leader asked, as the other two continued to laugh and record my every move. I kept my head down, so they would think I was still crying. I glanced back at Alexis, who was shaking her head no, but I was at a point of no return.

I walked straight up to the leader and chopped her in the throat. I countered my attack with two punches to her stomach that caused her to double over in pain. During my attack on the leader, I noticed the laughter came to a halt. I looked over at the girl that was standing next to the leader and she got in a fighting stance. I walked straight up to her and she swung as soon as I was within arm's reach. I got down low and came up with a fierce uppercut that knocked her off her feet. I could hear ooohs and aaaahs in the distance. When I looked at the third girl, she started to back away. "Don't run now, scary bitch!" I heard someone yell in the crowd.

"Listen, it was their idea," she said nervously with both hands in the hair. I shook my head slowly as I walked up to her. She turned around to run but her long jet black weave betrayed her. When she turned, I was able to grab it and pull her to me in a "Get over here" motion like Scorpion in Mortal Combat.

She bucked around and slipped on some trash. She hit the floor with a loud thud and it knocked the wind out of her. I chopped her in the throat and stood to my feet. Surprisingly, I was able to control myself. I knew that if I continued on with my assault, I would be in jail on three counts of murder. I bent over and took something out of each of their purses to remember them by, then gestured for Alexis to come on.

"I'm so proud of you Nessa," she beamed. I looked at her with a side eye as we headed home.

## Phat

I sat in my room thanking God Frankie was still alive after we finished counting all that damn money. I don't care about Vanessa making us think she was dead first because I know she wouldn't have if Boss Lady's men weren't there. Now, I know you're thinking "Why that nigga let Chris knock his ass out like that?" Well shit, a nigga real live felt like I deserved it. I started to fight back and I know I can whoop his ass but at the time, I thought my sister was dead and had she died, it would have been my fault. Now, if you were thinking "How this nigga forget about the toy chest?" I can't even answer that shit because in all honesty, it was as simple as forgetting. Shit, I was just glad Chris reminded me by asking about it and even more glad when he and Alexis helped me count it.

Alexis texted me after her and Vanessa made it to the mall and told me about Vanessa suggesting we buy an island for us and just chill. Shit, that would be so perfect. We'd be away from the bullshit and I'd keep Alexis barefoot and pregnant in the kitchen without worrying about not being with them because I didn't make it back from a rocky job.

I tried to wait up for them but shit, by hour three, a nigga was dog tired. I have no idea how far along Alexis is but it seems like since I found out, I'm always tired. I would say tired and horny, but I've always been always horny. That's why meeting Alexis was the best thing that ever happened to me since her sexual appetite is just as strong as mine, if not stronger.

I walked to the back of the house to check on Frankie and she was knocked out. I could tell she wasn't sleeping peacefully because of the frown etched on her face. If that wasn't a dead giveaway, then the sweat was. I wanted to wake her up but the last time I woke her up, she jumped up shooting, so I left her in her room.

When I walked back in my room, the hairs on the back of my neck stood up instantly. I looked around the room but I didn't see anyone. I looked under the bed, in my bathroom, and in the closet. I walked over to the window and as soon as I moved the curtains, I saw someone duck off. Rage filled my body as I took off. I ran through the living room and out the door. The girls had been gone so long, it was starting to get dark.

"What's going on?" Chris asked, once we made it to the back of the house. I didn't know that he followed me outside when I ran passed him.

"Man, I thought I saw somebody," I said, as I rubbed my hand across my head in exasperation.

"In your room?" Chris asked. His question jogged my memory as I nodded my head.

"Yea man, that shit just happened to me in your room, remember?" he asked, as he eyes searched the property for any movement. I started to search too but I couldn't see anyone.

I shook my head as we made our way back inside. A nigga ain't even tired no more.

**Chris**

After Vanessa and Alexis left, I got on Vanessa's laptop to see what all she had found out about Donna Walters. It looked like her search was based solely on Remy Bleu and that's fine, but what if something happens that causes Donna not to show up to the event. I've noticed that I'm good at computers but I hadn't told anyone. I guess I never knew because I hadn't had much access to them in my life but I find it simple to use. I used Vanessa's laptop to find out everything I could about Donna Walters. I was able to figure out her address, birthday, and I had access to her bank records. She'd been getting large sums of money deposited for every two weeks for the last five years. As crazy as it is, even with all of the deposits, she only has $4,000 available right now. For the last four years, I see she's been paying Steven's Security Company, so now I know she has security protecting her.

"Man fuck!" I said out loud to myself once I noticed a raise in pay this year alone to the same security company. That means some shit happened to her that made her beef up her security guards. Now, we going to have to take a different approach. I don't even know what approach Vanessa wants to take, being as though all she said was she wants to try some shit. After a few hours of finding out as much information as I could about Donna, I was even more confused about how we would get to her. Shit seemed impossible.

I left out of Vanessa's room and headed into the living room to watch TV. The TV ended up watching me though because before I knew it, I was sleep.

*****

The door opening caused me to jump out of my sleep. As soon as I opened my eyes, I saw Phat run out the door. I hopped up and ran behind him, in case he needed my help. I wasn't the least bit surprised when he thought he saw someone watching him from his window since the shit had just happened to me. That just adds to one more thing that we have to worry about while killing the rest of these people.

We headed back inside and I hopped in the shower, so I wouldn't be the one everybody was waiting on when it was time to go. I threw on something simple because really, niggas can wear anything and it will look good, as long as their shoes clean. Once I finished getting dressed and walked into the living room, Phat looked at me crazy. "What man? I'm tryna be ready so we can get this over with. Shit, we wasted all day to kill one bitch," I said and took a seat on the couch.

"You right man. Tomorrow, we need to split up and knock three of them out. Boss Lady ain't gone know what to do," he said, hyped up. Well, I could tell he was hyped because I know him but if you would have seen him, you would have thought he was just talking.

I watched him head to the back to get dressed as I thought about Vanessa's dad. Maybe it's him that's been watching us but why would he be watching us? Well shit, it's not even really us; it's more so Phat or Alexis.

About thirty minutes later, Alexis and Vanessa came walking in the house. "What's that smell?" I asked with a frown on my face. Vanessa ignored me and walked straight to the back. Alexis tossed me her truck keys. "Nooo, I get to push the whip?" I asked because Alexis never lets anyone drive her truck.

"Fuck no nigga, get her bags out the car!" she snapped and headed to her new favorite place in the house, the kitchen.

It took me two trips to get all of her shit in the house. I had bags all up my arms as I carried them in the house. I was trying to make one trip but that proved to be harder than I thought it would be. When I carried everything to her room, I could hear the shower running so she must be getting ready as well.

Phat and I walked into the living room at the same time. He laughed at the fact that Alexis was eating ice cream with Ruffle chips smashed in it. Shit looked nasty as fuck to me but she was munching like it was the best thing known to man.

"So, what's up with Vanessa?" I asked. I watched her pause dramatically before she scooped more ice cream in her mouth. She gave us a quick rundown of what happened at the mall and I can understand why she came in the house pissed off. In the short amount of time I've known Vanessa, I know this shit ain't over though.

"Ya'll, I was so proud of her because I thought she was going to kill em!" Alexis said, as she swallowed more ice cream. I watched her eat in amazement because I had never seen anyone eat ice cream that fast without getting a brain freeze. We continued talking until Vanessa came out the room trying to get Alexis' attention. She was so engrossed in eating her ice cream and running her mouth that she didn't notice Vanessa standing in the hallway.

I stood to my feet and headed towards her. She was looking sexy as fuck in some black laced boy shorts with a half bra to match. I allowed my eyes to travel her slim body and when I made it to her face, she was frowning. "What your problem?" I asked with a smile.

"I wanted Lexi," she pouted, as she crossed her arms over her chest.

"Well, I know more about women looking like money than she do. Let's go," I said, as I walked passed her in her room. She sucked her teeth and followed me inside and closed the door.

"So, check this out. I found out everything you need to know to work your moves on Donna," I said to her. I paused because her jaw instantly hit the floor.

"What you mean work my moves?" she asked with a worried expression on her face.

"She's gay baby and has a lot of security. Only you will be able to get passed them if she wants you," I explained. She stood in front of me with a confused expression on her face. "I told you I found out everything there is to know about Donna Walters. Your search was more focused on Remy," I said, as I hopped on her bed.

"Oh, ya'll on first name basis now huh?" she asked with a smile tugging at her lips. She was trying to fake an attitude. I ignored her and hopped down to look through her clothes. "What are you looking for?" she asked.

"Something sexy. Go do your hair or something," I said, as I continued to go through her clothes. She sucked her teeth and pulled the ball she had in her head out. I looked back and had to do a double take. I could tell her hair was wet and it had a slight wave to it that made her look exotic with her boy shorts on. Her hair is so long that I couldn't see the bra anymore. I stared at her as she put lotion on her long toned legs. She must have felt me looking at her because she started smiling.

"You gone stare or come help?" she asked, as she looked directly at me. I knew what she really wanted me to do and I want to do it too, but we have moves to make.

"Baby, if I come over there right now, we won't be going to the party and we already wasted a day that could have been spent killing," I said, as I tore my eyes away from her little sexy ass. I promise she's the first slim chick I've ever been attracted to and she got ya boy gone!

I found a long black dress that just so happened to be made the way her bra is except it drops really low in the back. I stared at it for a minute because I couldn't believe she picked this out. She's normally on her tom boy swag and she looks cute, but I've never seen her like this before. "Alexis must have grabbed this?" I asked, as I held it up for her to see. She nodded her head as she squeezed her hair together in her fist while she put some white stuff on it.

I stared on because I was confused but whatever she calls what she is doing is making her hair curly. "What are you doing?" I asked when she was almost done with it.

"I don't like using heat and my hair has a natural curl to it. I use mousse to keep the curl without the freeze," she explained. I still had no idea what the hell she was talking about but it's sexy as fuck.

I grabbed the dress and walked up behind her. I unsnapped her bra and let it fall to floor. I slid my thumb from the nape of her neck down her spine and stopped where her boy shorts started. She let out a soft moan that made my dick rock up immediately. "You sexy as fuck ma," I whispered hoarsely in her ear. I was fighting with myself mentally because I wanted to bend her over right now, but we need to get this shit over with. I laid the dress on the bed and some all black heels to go with it and left the room.

I headed back in the living room and Alexis started laughing. "What's funny?" I asked.

"She didn't give you none, huh?" she asked before she pointed at my dick and started laughing again. Phat threw a pillow at me with a disgusted look on his face as I turned my back on them. It had already started to go down, so I walked in the kitchen and fixed me a glass of water as I thought about killing Steve. I couldn't wait to get my hands on that rat ass nigga!

About fifteen minutes later, Vanessa came strutting out of the room and my jaw hit the floor. The dress was beautiful but on Vanessa's body, it was stunning. She walked real slow, like maybe she couldn't walk in the heels or something, but she looked good. I didn't realize how revealing the dress was but I was just glad she was going to be coming home with me after tonight.

**Vanessa**

As I slid into the dress, I didn't really know how it went. When Chris first laid it on the bed, I thought it looked really simple but it wasn't. "Yeah, Alexis definitely threw this one in without me noticing," I said out loud to myself. When I pulled it all the way up, I almost tore the clear strap that goes on my back like a tube top dress. My entire back was on display and luckily I have small breasts because the split in the front would tell it all on a big breasted woman. At this very moment, I wish I had my belly button pierced because the split started between my breasts and flowed all the way down to my waist line, so my belly button was visible. I slid my feet into the heels and took a minute to get my balance because this is literally my first time wearing heels. My neck felt bare but luckily Alexis ran in the jewelry store and loaded up on accessories.

I rummaged through the bags until I found the bag with the jewelry in it and chose the plain one that was silver with three diamonds on the charm. It had earrings to match, so I put those on as well. I pulled my now curly hair out of my face slightly and used hair pins to push it all to one side. When I looked in the mirror, I couldn't believe I was staring at myself. I now look better than the people that talk bad about me. Shit, if I dressed nice more often, I probably wouldn't be so insecure. I grabbed my Aquafina lip balm and applied it to my lips before I headed out my room door with my brand new black clutch.

As I walked down the hall slowly, all I could think about was not falling. It felt like I was gliding because I was concentrating so hard on not being on the ground. The first person I locked eyes with was Chris and he had never looked at me like that before. His gaze was so intense that it caused me to blush and look away from him. When I looked at Alexis, she stood up and started dancing and singing, "That's my best friend, that's my best friend, flexin! Big ole booty bitch missus from Texas, what's next is? I'm gone skeet off, lil nigga come catch me, catch me.

And that's my bestie, my bestie, my best friend, go best friend!"
She danced and sang Young Thug's song.

When she opened her eyes, we were all looking at her. I had a
smile on my face and when she looked at me, we both filled the
room with laughter. *Yea I'm the shit*, I thought to myself as I
walked into the living room. "Let's go ya'll because we gotta
stop at Walgreens," I said, as we headed out the door. I heard
someone grab some keys but I didn't know who until Phat
hopped in the driver's seat.

*****

*At the lounge*
The lounge was packed but everybody seemed to be having a
good time. I felt nothing but good vibes around me. "Too bad I
gotta shake shit up," I said out loud to myself. I headed to the bar
and ordered a shot of Patron.

"I got it," a sexy chocolate guy said that was sitting next to me.
He stared at me so long, I know he was imagining me naked and
bent over this bar right now.

"Naw, no da fuck you don't patna!" Chris snapped, as he slid
between us.

"We're on a job," I said through clenched teeth only for his ears.

I smiled softly at the bartender, who sat my shot in front of me.
"I don't even like men," I said before I downed my shot. The
only reason I said that is because Donna Walters had just taken a
seat two chairs over from me. "Can I get another one please?" I
asked, as I did my best act of seduction by licking salt off the rim
of the glass. I grabbed the lime and sucked as hard as I could
without making an unattractive face. I glanced at Chris and his
mouth was wide open. *We can't bring him when I'm being
seductive*, I thought to myself as I laughed softly. I looked to my
right and had a clear view of Donna Walters. I smirked slightly
because she was already looking at me.

I grabbed my bank card out of my clutch to set my trap. I waited until the bartender was back in front of me before I slid the card across the bar. "I'm going to buy the bar," I said. "Oh and I need a V.I.P section and two bottles of Patron," I said, as I stood to my feet. I waited patiently for a waitress to escort me to my section. Once I was in my section, I sat back and enjoyed myself by simply watching other people have fun.

"Who are you?" someone asked with a camera in her hand.

"Who's asking?" I asked with my interest piqued.

"Jasmine Taylor. I'm a blogger," she said with a smile.

"Aw crap, I left my bitch be gone spray at home," I said to her. She looked confused as I poured myself another shot. When I looked up, she was still standing there. "Bitch be gone!" I yelled over the music as I threw my shot in her face. She gasped for air and fanned her eyes as she stormed away. She probably couldn't see because the liquor got in her eyes.

I smiled to myself as I sat back and poured another shot. "You treat all the ladies like that?" a high pitched voice asked. When I looked up, it was Donna Walters. I forced a smile because I could tell shit just got that much harder to do because of her high ass voice.

"Only the ones that are unwanted," I said with a slight smile. I downed the shot and winked at her, and she strolled right on in my section and took a seat next to me. I checked my clutch to make sure what I needed was still there.

"You smell so good beautiful," she said, as she leaned closer to me. I down another shot to help relax because my body was as stiff as a board. I allowed her to rub her hand up and down my back softly, even though it made me itch. I'm sure what she was doing was supposed to feel good but it didn't. I don't know if it's because I'm not gay or if she's just doing it wrong or something.

*When I'm with you* by Tony Terry began to play and she asked me to dance. She was way taller than me, so I threw my hands as close to her neck as I could as we slow dance in my VIP section. I closed my eyes and imagined she was Chris as her hands roamed my body. My imagination definitely did not come into handy at this moment and no matter how hard I tried, I just couldn't imagine that she was Chris.

"Fuck!" I said out loud to myself.

"What's wrong?" she asked, as she looked down at me. If it wasn't for her eyes and teeth, I'd think I was dancing with Casper the friendly ghost as black as she is.

"Um... nothing," I stammered. She took a step away from me and I know this is my only chance to get her. "Being near you excites me. It's been awhile," I said, as I looked at her bashfully.

"How about I show you what I can do for you?" she asked, as she grabbed my hand like she knew I wouldn't say no. I grabbed my clutch on our way out of VIP and into the bathroom.

As soon as we made it in the bathroom, she locked the door and attacked. Not physically, well not in a violent way, although I felt violated in a major way. She licked and kissed roughly all over my neck and chest. I felt like bugs were all over me and I couldn't wait until I was able to go home and wash her filth off of me. She groped my breasts with so much force; they started to throb. She gripped my butt and brought me closer to her as she tried to kiss me in the mouth. I turned my head just in time and she landed on my cheek. She ignored what I did and allowed her tongue to travel to my ear. She moaned loudly in my ear, like I was doing something to her. I stood as stiff as a board waiting on my opportunity to strike. This is not how I expected to spend my first night out.

She used her hands to place my arms around her but I let them fall to my side. "What's wrong?" she asked in between sloppy kisses on my neck. I could smell her breath in her slob and I wanted to vomit so bad.

"I like being in control," I managed to force out pass the vomit that was threatening to come up.

"What you want me to do?" she asked, as she got on her knees in front of me. I looked at her strangely as she bowed her head waiting on my command.

I reached in my clutch and grabbed the syringe with a needle attached to it that I bought from Walgreens on my way here. "Close your eyes and don't open them!" I said.

"Yes master," she replied, shocking the fuck out of me.

"Bitch, did I tell you to talk?" I asked, jumping into character. She didn't respond. "Answer me!" I yelled.

"No master, you did not ask me to talk," she said, without looking up at me. I smiled a real smile for the first time since I laid eyes on her.

I got on my knees next to her and pushed her head to the side roughly. I needed to see her veins. "You've been a bad girl," I said to her like I was talking to a child. The whole time I slid my finger across her neck, trying to find a good vein to use. I thumped her neck when I found the perfect one and she flinched. "Don't move again!" I threatened. I stared at her vein for several seconds and put the needle as close to it as possible without actually touching her. I took a deep breath and stuck the needle in her vein and pushed air inside.

She looked up at me in shock as her hand went directly up to her neck. "Wh... what..." she tried to get out but she couldn't. She fell all the way over on the floor gasping for air. All of a sudden, she clutched her chest and rocked slightly back and forth. Her facial expression was twisted, making it appear that she was in excruciating pain. I stood there as silent as a church mouse until she took her last breath. I waited two minutes, stuck my needle in my clutch, and ran out of the bathroom.

I ran smack dab into two big bulky guys dressed in three piece suits. "Help me! C'mon, you gotta help!" I yelled, then grabbed one of their hands and led him into the bathroom.

"What the fuck happened?" he asked.

"We were getting busy, and she fell out and grabbed her chest," I said, forcing myself to breathe heavily as if I was panicking. I looked passed him and saw a trickle of blood on her neck where I stuck the needle in too hard. I could feel my breathing speed up on its own, along with my heart rate. I stood there silently praying that he didn't notice the blood on her neck. He turned around to look at her and I prepared to run. When he turned back to me, he slid me a knot of money and I gave him a confused look.

"Keep what happened here to yourself. We're gonna take her home and make it appear as if the heart attack happened there," he explained. I nodded my head and exited the bathroom. I went straight to the bar to get my ID and signaled for the guys to come on, so we could go home.

On the way home, I filled them in on everything that transpired in the bathroom and for the third time tonight, Chris' jaw hit the floor. Phat shook his head. "That's some shit there," Phat said, as he continued to drive.

"I'm hungry as fuck," Chris said.

"Don't stop. I need to shower," I said with a frown.

"Man, you stopped and got Wendy's after I had just got tortured and was laying in the backseat damn near dead!" he snapped at me.

"But did you die?" I asked and Phat laughed. We stopped and got food, then headed back to the house.

When we pulled up, there was one black van parked outside. I got out the car and noticed Aurel and another guy standing on the porch. "Why are you out here?" I asked, simply because they're normally inside.

"She no open door," Aurel said. I could see that he was upset about that from the look on his face.

"Yea because she's home alone," I said. We unlocked the door to enter and they followed suit.

"Boss Lady like how you work. Good job. You each get $30,000," he said, as they left as quickly as they had come.

"I can get use to this," I said, as I headed to my room.

"Well don't!" Chris yelled at my back.

I walked to the back to check on Frankie but she wasn't in her room. I checked all over the house but she wasn't inside. "Fuck, where's Frankie?" I asked, as I ran back in the living room.

## Frankie

*Mrs. Anderson had four foster children: Allison, Marisa, Antwan, and myself. She was told by doctors years ago that she wouldn't be able to bear children, well at least that was what she told us. Anyway, miraculously, one day she was feeling sick and her husband, who was home after being discharged dishonorably, took her to the doctor and found out she was pregnant. She had a horrible pregnancy but gave birth to a healthy, mentally sick individual and named him Prodigy. Prodigy and Antwan both had their own rooms. I shared a room with Allison and Marisa.*

*Every night, Prodigy would sneak in our room and mess with either Allison or Marisa. He never touched me because he said I looked like a boy, and he was no punk. Allison was 15 and Marisa was 13, so their bodies were developing and betraying them at the same time. Time was not on their sides at all as their bodies blossomed more and more. At the time, I had no idea what it was called that he was doing but I knew it was wrong. It looked painful but I dared not to intervene. Both Allison and Marisa stopped talking to me because I never helped them fight him off. As sad as it may sound, I was just glad it wasn't happening to me.*

*I snuck off to bed early, in hopes that I would fall asleep before Prodigy came in to do those things he does to Allison and Marisa, so they wouldn't expect me to help. I laid in my bed sweating profusely because the air conditioner was broken and it was summer time. I had stripped all the way down to just my t-shirt and panties when the room door opened. I looked at the door and there stood Prodigy with the same look in his eyes that he has every night. Allison and Marisa trailed in slowly behind him. I shook my head slowly because I was not able to fall asleep before their time came.*

*I watched with tears in my eyes as Allison and Marisa climbed in their twin sized beds and waited for what was bound to come.*

*Neither of them looked at me but I'd gotten use to the cold shoulder. The thought that tonight was my turn never occurred to me, not even as I watched Prodigy make his way to my bed. My body started to tremble as he pulled my small dirty cover off my body. "W... w... wh... what are you doing?" I asked with a shaky voice, although I knew to a certain extent what was next.*

*"Scoot over," he said, as he ignored my question. I shook my head no as my body continued to shake.*

*He pushed me roughly and I jumped out of bed. I was not about to lay willingly like Allison and Marisa. "Don't fight and it won't hurt so bad," Marisa said to me. I looked at her as if she had lost her mind and Allison needed to help her find it. I'd been through enough and this was not about to be added to my list.*

*"Get back over here," he said, as he patted the place next to him on my bed. I shook my head no and watched how anger filled his body instantly. He jumped up and lunged at me. I moved just in time and he collided with the wall behind me with a loud thud.*

*I grabbed Marisa and Allison's hands and pulled them towards the door because we had to get out of there. I ran dead into Mrs. Anderson. "Where do you think you're going?" she snarled with her chubby hand on her plump hip.*

*"Prodigy. He keeps touching them and tonight, he tried to touch me," I explained in a rushed tone. Whap! Mrs. Anderson smacked me so hard across my face, I stumbled into the wall. Marisa and Allison scurried back into our room and closed the door behind them. I guess they rather face Prodigy instead of Mrs. Anderson.*

*"You're lucky my boy looked at you, you maggot!" she screamed, as she swung at me again. I expected it that time and ducked just in time. Her fist crashed into the wall as I ran around her.*

*I ran straight for the front door but didn't have the key to get out. She had the type of deadbolt that requires a key on both sides. I turned back around with sweat dripping all over my body. Fresh tears stung my eyes as they slid down my cheeks blending with the sweat. My face stung slightly from the slap Mrs. Anderson delivered moments ago. I watched in fear as she waddled down the hall towards me.*

"Shit!" I said, as I jumped out of my sleep. Lately, every time I went to sleep, I ended up reliving a terrible memory. I slid out of my bed and went to take a shower. My body was drenched in sweat. My chest and ribs hurt like hell but I refused to stay in bed while everybody else work together as a team. Sure, Alexis isn't working with them but I'm sure if she wasn't pregnant, she would be working with them too.

After I finished my shower, I threw on one of my black jogging suits. I pulled my hood over my head as I did my best to sneak out of the house. I peeked in the room Alexis shares with Phat and saw she was knocked out. I guess that baby has been kicking her and Phat's ass, since they sleep a lot more now. As I passed Chris' room, I peeked in and noticed he was still gone. I let out a deep breath once I made it to the living room. *Everybody's gone,* I thought to myself. I walked in the kitchen and grabbed my car keys and headed out the door.

As I walked to my car, I looked around to make sure nobody was watching me or about to pull up. I pulled off and headed to The Gadget Shop. I bought three tracking devices and headed back to the car and drove back home. Once I was home, I ran quickly in the house and got Vanessa's notebook to write her a letter. Once I was done, I activated two of the tracking devices. I put both remotes on her nightstand and labeled them both. I slid one of them in my pocket and carried the other one back out with me to the car along with some supplies I may need later.

I pulled out the yard and parallel parked and shut the engine off. About an hour or so later, one of Boss Lady's black vans pulled in. I waited patiently for them to enter our house like they always do but they didn't go in. "Fuck!" I cursed under my breath. I made sure the overhead light was off so when I opened the car door to get out, it wouldn't come on. I slid out of the car slowly without closing the door behind me.

I stayed low to the ground as I crab walked to the van. I slid my body underneath the van and taped the tracking device to a pipe under the van. I made sure it was on and crab walked back to my car. I slid in without being detected. The first part of my mission was complete.

I waited patiently for Vanessa, Chris, and Phat to pull up and when they did, I began to wish I had some kind of way to give them a signal. The letter should be enough but I know they're going to be worried until they find the letter. Out of the corner of my eye, I could see someone creeping along the side of the house heading towards the back. I wanted to let them know what I saw but my cellphone was inside and I couldn't say anything without Boss lady's men knowing I'm alive. "Being dead sucks!" I said out loud, as I watched the person creep off until they were out of view. I'm not a fighter like Vanessa, so I would only cause more problems if I chase whoever that is down.

I waited until the transaction with the money was complete before I cranked my car up. I watched them back out of the parking spot and pull away. I followed them with my lights off until we got on the highway, then I turned my lights on. It took them about an hour to turn off onto a rocky road and I continued going straight. I made a U-turn and when I got to that road, I cut my lights off and drove slowly. I drove for about thirty minutes before I saw what looked like an iron gate. I began to grin from ear to ear because we are finally one step ahead of this bitch.

I parked my car but left the engine running as I hopped out and did a light jog through the trees up to the gate. I saw guards everywhere and it made the smile wipe off my face instantly. "Fuck, how do I get in?" I said out loud to myself.

"You don't," a familiar voice said from behind me.

**Chris**

Vanessa was freaking the fuck out because she couldn't find Frankie. I understand she's worried, but Frankie is grown and is going to do whatever the hell she wants to do. I could tell Vanessa's antics was pissing Alexis off from the scowl etched on her face. She sat on the couch next to Phat and watched Vanessa pace back and forth as she tried to figure out where Frankie could have gone.

She stopped pacing and ran to the box and pulled out the four pictures that were left. "Fuck!" she said, as she threw the pictures back in the box.

"What?" I asked confused.

"I thought maybe she was gone to do a hit," she said with her head hung low. Alexis got up and walked to the back and walked up behind Vanessa. A few seconds after she hugged her, Vanessa's weight fell on Alexis. I jumped up and grabbed Vanessa, and Phat grabbed Alexis.

Vanessa dangled in my arms, she was out like a light as I dropped down to my knees. I felt a tightness in my chest as I looked at her. "She's going to be ok," Alexis said. It wasn't until I looked at her and saw a needle in her hand that what had happened registered in my brain. "She will be out for the rest of the night but that gives us all a chance to rest. Frankie will be fine," she said, like she knew something we didn't. "Tomorrow, when she wakes up, we can tell her Frankie will be back later. Say she went to the store or something so ya'll can be focused on the last four people on the list. The faster that is taken care of, the faster we can get back to ourselves," she said then left out of the living room.

I looked at Phat, who shrugged at me because he didn't know what was going on either. I carried Vanessa to my bed and returned to the living room with Phat. "What's going on bruh?" I asked him.

"Man, I don't know man but I heard Alexis on the phone with Wayne," Phat said, as he ran his hand across his head.

"Nessa's brother?" I asked. Phat nodded his head. "Da fuck were they talking bout?" I asked with a slight frown. It's getting harder and harder to trust any damn body these days. Phat shook his head.

I got up and went to the bed wondering what the fuck is going on.

*****

*The next day*

When I woke up, it felt like I was being watched. I jumped up and calmed down when I realized the person that was watching me was Vanessa. "What the fuck did Alexis give me last night and why?" she asked with an unwavering stare. I stared back at her, thinking of what Alexis told me to tell her. This is the woman I love, the woman I plan to spend the rest of my life with, so I can't leave her in the dark.

"C'mere," I said, as I looked at her. She shook her head no as she crossed her hands over her chest.

"Get yo hard headed ass over here now!" I snapped at her. She sucked her teeth, rolled her eyes, and walked over to me. "I need to enlighten you on something I tried to tell you last night but got distracted," I said. I watched her body tense up and shook my head. "Nothing hurtful, crazy ass girl," I said to her. Her body remained as stiff as a board. "Phat and I both have been seeing someone watching us from outside of his window. Whenever we go out to see, we can't find nobody," I said to her. She hopped up and tried to run but I grabbed the back of her pants and pulled her back on the bed.

She grunted her aggravation and rolled her eyes. "We need to put everything on the table before you go all mighty mouse on us!" I snapped at her. She was getting on my damn nerves with this rah rah shit she be pulling.

"Well, let's all sit in the living room," she said and hopped out the bed. This time, I allowed her to walk away without grabbing her. I climbed out the bed and followed her to the living room where Alexis and Phat were already seated. Oddly, they weren't next to each other the way they normally are. "Why ya'll on opposite sides of the universe?" Vanessa asked. Leave it to Vanessa to ask some shit everybody else would have ignored.

"Because daddy dearest thinks I'm cheating on him with Wayne," Alexis said, then made a face at Phat. He sighed heavily but didn't respond to the petty nature most women have.

"My Wayne? My brother that's fucking your sister, April?" Vanessa asked, and Alexis' facial expression was one for the books.

"How did you know? Don't tell him I told you because he wanted to tell you," Alexis said. It was like the tension in the room dissipated immediately.

"Girl, they been messing around since we were younger. That's why he never wanted me to come to your house. He tried to make it about Jerry but I figured out April talk a lot," Vanessa said with a shrug. "So, go on over dea chile!" Vanessa said, mocking someone's granny. We all laughed, including Phat, as Alexis got up and sat next to him then laid her head on his chest.

"April's pregnant," Alexis blurted out.

"Noooo!" Vanessa said excitedly. I sat back and watched their exchange for about five more minutes before I got pissed off.

"Man, no offense, but fuck all that. We got business to handle and Frankie to find!" I snapped. "Don't ask me no fucking questions at all! I got something to run down to ya. Frankie gone and we don't know where da fuck she went, and we can't worry bout dat right now. Ya'll gotta know she can handle herself. Somebody been watching either Phat or Alexis, and we keep missing who it is. It could be someone watching for Boss Lady or it could Nessa's dad," I paused to let everything sink in as I made my way to the box. I gave Vanessa number seven, Phat number eight, and I held on to number nine.

"Give me one," Alexis said with a pout. I shot a glance at Phat, who shook his head, so I placed the last one in the box. I handed everyone the tape recorders.

"I say we split up and knock these out, so we can get them over with. Keep your phones on ya and send a text after you complete your hit," I said. I stood and waited for someone to ask a question but everybody appeared to be lost in their own thoughts. I walked off to my room to get ready for my hit. I sat in the chair next to my bed and hit play.

"Hey Sweetheart. We're quickly coming to a close I see and you only have one more left after this one before we get to meet. The picture of this sexy hunk of meat is Cameron Black. He's an entrepreneur and he's great at what he's selling. Ha! Anyway, if you flip the picture over, there are a list of places he frequents daily with the time he normally goes. You should also see his home address. Yes, I did all the work for you and you can thank me later! Anywho, he helped me with something and found out too much information along the way. You know what they say baby, loose lips sink ships. $100,000 for this loose end. Toodles." The tape ended.

I sat in my chair confused about how easy all of these people have been to kill and I'm wondering what the hell is really going on. I stood up and threw on some jean pants and a crisp black t-shirt with my all black Air Force Ones. I checked the time and it was almost lunch time. On Saturdays, he meets Alicia at the

Heat Bag for lunch, so I headed in that direction. When I walked through the living room, nobody was there. I grabbed my keys and left.

*****

*At the Heat Bag*
I pulled up to the restaurant and spotted Cameron and Alicia as soon as I entered. I took a seat in the back by the restroom. All of the tables went in the same direction but luckily for me, his back was to me. I sat in the back patiently eating some complimentary noodles as I waited on the perfect time to make my move. I wanted to go ahead and get it over with but I didn't want to rush it. I have no idea how I'm going to kill him at all. This is winging it at its best!

A few minutes later, those noodles were running through me. I quickly checked around for cameras and when I didn't see any, I ducked inside the bathroom. *Guess I'm gonna have to catch him another time*, I thought to myself, as I put the toilet protector down. I'm not even going to tell you what I did next because I'm pretty sure that's an image you'd rather not have at this moment.

After I finished using the bathroom, I realized it was one of those automatic toilets that flush when you get up but it didn't. I was looking all over that damn toilet trying to find a button to flush it but I didn't see one. I started waving my hand by the toilet, in case it missed my motion when I stood up. Then I saw a sign right above the toilet and it said out of order. I shook my head and stepped completely out the stall to wash my hands.

"Ooooweee, somebody lit it up!" someone said, as soon as they entered the bathroom.

"Hell yea, man, funky mufucker!" I said with an attitude. I looked up in the mirror and had to do a double take because Cameron Black was the guy talking. I dried my hands off as he opened the stall I just came out of.

"Oooh shit!" he said, as he backed away from the stall. His back was to me, so I took that as my chance to punch him as hard as I could in the back of his head.

I was shocked beyond measure when he stumbled forward, dropped down to his knees, and his head fell in the toilet. I could feel the vomit rising but I had to suppress it to complete the task at hand. "Fuck it," I said out loud to myself as I entered the stall with him. I turned around and sat on his shoulders, so I could put all of my weight on him. The goal was to drown him and be done with it. The first few seconds were easy, then he started jerking and swinging his arms. The only thing he was hitting was the porcelain toilet in front of him. I sent a silent prayer that none of the shit splashed on me as I put my feet on both sides of the stall. I pressed down hard until he stopped thrashing around.

I put my legs down and continued to sit on him for a few more minutes, just to catch my breath. I stood up, turned around, and shook my head at how this man spent his last moments. "Man, life has a way of throwing shit your way," I said, as I exited the bathroom then the restaurant.

I headed on home to collect my $100,000 for this hit.

**Vanessa**

I sat in the living room after everyone left to do their own thing. Chris went to his room first, then Alexis followed Phat to their room. I'm pretty sure she's pissed that she doesn't get to do the last one but it's for two pretty damn good reasons. For one, she's pregnant, which should be enough of a reason all together, but since it isn't, the fact that she's never killed anyone is another reason. I don't even know why Chris looked to Phat for the answer because I wasn't going to let her do it either. Hell, nobody should have to stop her from doing anything stupid any damn way.

I clutched the tape recorder in my hand as I stared at the picture with the number 7 on it. It was a picture of Samantha Wells. I stared at her picture and wondered how she and Boss Lady crossed paths. I could tell Samantha was once a beautiful girl but whatever her drug of choice is has taken her down through there. I sat back against the couch and pressed play.

"Hey Sweetheart. Baby girl, you're on a roll! Ok, the dope fiend you're looking at is Samantha Wells. She used to work for me in the kitchen, if you know what I mean. She was my favorite chef and the only one who could whip it and cut it just right while stretching it out for me. Well, come to find out, she was stretching it out farther than I thought she was and getting high off my supply! Major no-no in my line of business. You can find her where you left those three thugs who were gonna have their way with you. Heroine has become the reason she lives and breathes. Use it to take her breath away. I've already prepared a hot shot and it's in your mailbox ripe for the taking. $50,000 Good luck." The tape ended.

"Damn," I said out loud to myself. I had no idea she knew about the three guys I killed a while back in the projects. That same day I met the smoker, Kim, that helped me place the ad for my newfound business. I shook my head before I headed down memory lane, grabbed my keys, and headed out the door.

On the way over, I let my thoughts drift to my brother, Wayne. I hadn't seen him since I moved out and he hasn't tried to contact me at all. I guess it was because he was trying to keep a secret and I have a way of reading him like a book. Shit, I've always been able to get Wayne to do whatever I wanted him to do, no matter what it is. I remember the first time I asked him to let me kill a homeless person and he refused. All I did was tell him I wasn't his friend no more and we were off to find homeless people that wouldn't be missed.

It took about two hours for me to get to those projects. I parked at the same convenience store as I did last time. When I climbed out the car, I saw Jeremy playing dice with his friends in the same spot he was playing with them in the last time I was here. "Looking good ma," I heard someone say once I walked away. When I turned around, my cheeks flushed because it was Jeremy. I looked down at the outfit I had on. It was simple. I had on a peach colored crop top that said **love** across it in white letters. I wore black skinny jeans and a peach colored belt. I pulled my hair up into a high ponytail and the curls cascaded all over my face.

"Thanks," I said, as I turned my back to him and walked away. I touched my waist to make sure my stars were still in place and they were. I touched my back pocket to make sure the hot shot was still there and it was. I walked as slow as possible as my eyes scanned around for Samantha but I couldn't find her.

"Long time no see," a small smoker said, as she walked right up to me like she knew me. I crinkled up my nose because of her smell and I could only imagine what the rest of my face was doing. "Oh you done got some new clothes and you come back all cute and act like ueono no damn body!" she said, pointing her finger at my chest. I smiled when recognition set in.

"Heyyyy! I couldn't tell who you were when you first walked up. I'm sorry," I said apologetically. I was really happy to see her though. She helped me last time and I was hoping she would help me again.

"Watcha round here fo?" she asked, as she looked around.

"I'm looking for Samantha Wells. You know her?" I asked. I watched as Kim's eyes got big and she began to look around. "C'mon Kim, you know me. Help me out," I damn near pleaded.

"Watcha want wita?" she asked, as she looked me up and down.

"Kill her," I replied honestly. It was no point in lying to Kim; hell, she knows what I do for a living. A slow smile spread across her face as she started doing what I assumed is her happy dance.

"Gon' head gal, she right up dea. Second building apartment 3 second floor," she said with a big toothless grin.

"What she do to you?" I asked Kim with a smirk on my face.

"Bitch sucking up all da dicks better than me, so I gotta find other ways to make money," she said with a frown.

I dug in my pocket and gave her a twenty-dollar bill and walked off. "Be cafer," she said, as she headed towards the store. I headed down the road and up into the second building. The door creaked when I opened it and the smell of piss invaded my nostrils instantly. I placed my hand over my mouth, trying to suppress the urge to vomit. Shit, it's enough bodily fluids in this corridor any damn way.

I walked up the stairs after I made sure the guy posted up on the wall wasn't a threat. He looked like a corner boy and from the looks of things, I could tell I was the least of worries. If he was working for me, he most definitely would not be allowed to get head on the job. I could have easily been someone prepared to rob him or worse.

My face was balled into a tight disgusted scowl my entire walk up the flight of stairs. I can't imagine people living here that didn't have to. Hell, if I was that dope boy, I'd pay someone to clean up in here. I know after being in a pissy corridor all day, you're bound to leave smelling like piss.

I slowed my pace once I reached the second floor. I looked around slowly and noticed a really ugly, brown skinned guy standing outside of the apartment that I need to go in. He was about my height and had a permanent scowl on his face. I don't blame him though because if I was color purple ugly, I'd frown all the time too. *How am I gonna get around him?* I thought to myself.

"Seduction," I said softly. I swayed my small hips right up to him and got all in his personal space. The smell of cheese and corn chips radiated from his pores. He smiled a smelly smile until he saw the frown on my face.

"Da fuck yo problem?" he asked in a threatening tone. His breath smacked me in the face! It smelled like something crawled inside of him and died.

"Nothing," I said, as I tried to play it off with a forced smile but I could tell it was too late.

"Who you?" he asked with an attitude.

"Princess," I said after I wiped my face of all emotions. I was trying a nice approach but his funky ass wants to take me there.

"What you want?" he asked with a straight face. I couldn't read him but I could for damn sure smell him.

"Not what, who?" I answered him, as I teetered back and forth on the heels of my feet. I watched confusion wash over his face. "Fuck it," I said to myself because my approach clearly was not working out for me. I took a timid step back, jumped in the air, and kicked him in his chest. The blow caused him to hit the wall. He growled and charged at me. I dropped down low to the ground and did a spin kick that put him on his ass. I sat on his chest, pulled my knife out, and sliced his throat open.

I hopped up quickly to avoid getting blood on my clothes. I turned the doorknob and walked in, being careful to shut the door quickly behind me. "What you getting?" a guy asked, as soon as I closed the door.

"Hero," I said, as I scanned the room for my target.

He gave me a small sack just as I locked eyes with Samantha. I looked away to look inside the bag because I had never seen heroine before. I'm glad I'm not here to smoke it because I don't know how to change it to liquid form like the shot in my pocket. Samantha jumped up, clutching her chest, and pointing her finger at me. "Stay away Kathy!" she yelled. Confusion set in because I don't know why she thinks I'm Kathy. I began to wonder if she's referring to the same Kathy that my dad was talking to. That would mean that Boss Lady's name is Kathy.

"Aye, calm the fuck down!" the guy that handed me the drugs yelled.

"Keep her away," she said, watching my every move.

"What the fuck?" I said out loud to myself.

"Don't mind her. Find a seat," he said, then gave me a light shove.

I searched the small cramped place for an extra seat but couldn't find one. Just when I was about to give up, the smoker next to Samantha stood up slowly and walked towards me. I watched cautiously as he stumbled past me and headed for the door. I quickly sat next to Samantha but she didn't notice me because she had taken another shot. I slipped the hot shot out of my pocket and switched it out with hers. I wasn't sure if she was supposed to take the whole thing or what.

I stared at the tan colored liquid in the syringe until Samantha noticed it. I watched her eyes light up as she put her belt back on her arm. She pulled real tight, then stuck the needle in her arm. She only inserted a small portion of the drugs and allowed her head to lean to the side. I quickly reached over her and put the rest of the hot shot in her system. I watched her eyes roll to the back of her head. Her body started to shake and foam came out of her mouth. I could hear someone screaming in the hallway. When I looked back at Samantha, it looked like something out of the Exorcism. It freaked me out so bad, I started screaming.

The guy ran away from the door and over to me. I pointed frantically at Samantha and he just shook his head. I watched until her body stopped shaking and she sat on the couch dead with slob dripping down her chin. I shook my head and walked out of the apartment. The smoker that was seated next to Samantha was outside in the hallway going through the smelly guy's pocket and there was a lady slumped over on the wall. She must have saw the dead body, screamed, and the smoker knocked her out.

I left out of the smelly building and headed back to my car. "You got her?" Kim asked, coming out of nowhere.

I nodded my head and kept walking, then it dawned on me. I stopped and turned around and saw Kim was still standing there. "Hey Kim, you wouldn't by chance know a lady name Kathy, would you?" I asked, as I took a step in her direction. Kim began to fidget with a rubber band that she pulled from her wrist. "Kim," I called out to her. She looked up at me then looked away, which let me know she knows who Kathy is.

"Did you tell her about me killing those three guys?" I asked. I watch her nod her head nervously. "Do she come around here often?" I asked.

"She speaks to Jeremy and leaves. He hired you for those first couple of hits you did," she said with a sober tongue. She was sounding like the Kim I met the first time and not the drugged out Kim she was pretending to be when I first got here. I pulled more money from my pocket and handed it to her and she ran off.

I did a light jog to my car and drove home

## Phat

After Chris gave us our assignments, I got up and went to my room to listen to the tape. I sat down on the side of my bed, just as Alexis walked in the room with a frown on her face. "Why don't ya'll trust me to do the last hit?" she asked with her hands on her wide hips.

"Baby, it ain't got shit to do with trust! You ain't doing that shit pregnant!" I snapped at her.

"Would you let me if I wasn't pregnant?" she asked with a twist of her neck.

"Fuck no!" I said, as I frowned at her.

"Exactly, so why don't you trust me?" she asked. I see she just wants to argue about something and I'm not about to do this with her. We got two people left on this list and we will get Steve back, kill Boss Lady, and move far away; in that order. I don't have the time or the patience to deal with this bullshit right now.

I looked down at the tape recorder and pressed play. "Hey Baby doll I'm so excited about meeting you! The person you are looking at is Rodney Smith. He's a fat, useless, nothing ass nigga! I tried to help him Nessie! I tried to put him on game but nooo, he couldn't do a single job right because he was always drunk! What a fucking waste! His life has been spiraling out of control, ever since I cut him off but it all started with the bottle. He's been losing himself in it. Do me a favor for $60,000, drown him in his sorrows. Check on the side of the house in a red box and everything you will need is inside of it." The tape ended.

I looked up at Alexis and her mouth hung wide open. "What's wrong with you?" I asked because I could see the tears forming.

"That's her," she said, pointing at the tape recorder.

"That's who?" I asked confused.

"Nessa's mama. She's the only person that calls her Nessie," she said and climbed on the bed. I watched in silence as she pulled the covers over her body and snuggled against the pillows.

"I'm about to head out. You good?" I asked. I waited for her to nod her head before I left.

When I got outside, I saw the box immediately. It was so bright I began to wonder when they put it there because I'm sure I would have noticed it before now if it's been there. I picked it up and carried it to my car. I sat in the driveway and opened the box. It had an address, a bottle of Jack Daniels, and a funnel inside of it. I knew instantly what she wanted me to do.

I put the address in the GPS and followed the directions to get there. I wasn't surprised at all when I pulled into the parking lot of a bar. When I walked in, I spotted him immediately because he was arguing with the bartender about cutting him off. He stood up with an attitude and stormed passed me. He went to a pickup truck that was parked next to me and got in. I watched him fumble with his keys and began to wonder exactly how I should do what I needed to do.

I walked to my car and grabbed the bottle and funnel. "Aye, how about a drink for the road?" I suggested, as he dropped his keys again. The last thing he needed was another drink but I got to do what I got to do.

"Yea boy, see if you can hang," he slurred his words.

"How about a drinking game?" I asked and his eyes lit up. I walked around to the passenger's side of his car with the bottle and funnel.

"How you play?" he asked, as his head swayed from side to side.

"You just gotta drink without stopping. After you go, then I'll go, and whoever lasted the longest win money," I said and pulled out a knot of money and sat it on the dashboard. His eyes lit up when he saw the money.

"Ok, hold your head back," I said but he didn't respond. He had a glazed look in his eye as he stared off into space. I followed his line of vision but nobody was there.

"I'm ready," he said slowly, as he closed his eyes with a smile on his face. For some reason, I think he knows why I'm here and it's not to have a drinking game with him. He laid his head back against his seat and slouched his body down.

With shaky fingers, I slipped the funnel in his mouth as deep as it could go. He gagged slightly but he didn't put up any type of resistance. I twisted the top off the bottle and poured the contents in the funnel. His body jerked and he swung his arms wildly. I tightened my grip on the funnel and forced it deeper into his mouth. Some of the liquor bubbled up inside of the funnel mixed with blood as he continued to thrash about in his truck. A few minutes later, he stopped moving.

I shook my head and climbed slowly out of the pickup truck. I ripped the bottom half of my t-shirt and stuck it in the hole leading to his gas tank. I grabbed my lighter out of my pocket and lit the part of the shirt that was hanging out. I hopped in my car and pulled completely out of the parking lot and waited for the explosion. Once the truck was engulfed in flames, I headed back to the house.

**Alexis**

As I listened to Vanessa's mom call her Nessie on the tape, my blood began to boil. I was already pissed that they were treating me like some type of handicapped person or like they secretly thought I couldn't get the job done. Vanessa always has my back and it's about time I start having hers. I climbed in my bed and waited patiently for Phat to leave. I ducked in Chris' room and saw that he was gone and when I made it to the living room, so was Vanessa. "Perfect," I said out loud to myself. I grabbed the last picture and tape recorder and pressed play.

"Well done Baby Girl! The picture you are looking at is of Terrance Thomas. Baby, don't get distracted by his dark brown skin and light brown eyes like I did. He can't do anything right girl and he failed at the most important job I've ever given him! Then turned snitched! I've already done most of the work for you, so all you have to do is go to the address on the back of the picture and press the red button. When Aurel comes after this last hit to pay you, he will also have directions on how to get to my house, which is where we'll meet. $10,000." The tape ended.

I'm so fucking confused because I don't know if I need a gun or what's going to happen when I get to the address. I walked in Vanessa's room and saw she bought new gadgets and left them on her nightstand. I walked over to it and realized they were tracking devices and two of them were on. There was another one just sitting on the dresser with a remote and tracking device, so I grabbed it and turned it on. I left the remote on the dresser and slid the device in my pocket. I grabbed the machine gun out of the closet that she didn't know I knew she had and left.

I entered in my destination and set out to kill the last person. About an hour later, I pulled up to this sign that said enter here but there was no building. I hopped out of my truck and walked to the sign and saw a little door that looks like the cellar door at my grandma's house. I pulled it open and used my phone as a flashlight to guide my steps. I walked cautiously down the steps until I made it to the floor. I was completely out of breath by this time and had to bend over to catch it. I walked slowly through the spacious room I was in until I got to a pit.

"HELP ME!" a male voice screamed. I looked down into the pit and saw the man from the photo inside of it, so I started searching for the red button. As soon as I found it, I hit it without a second thought but nothing happened. I walked back over to the pit and saw that four slots opened inside of it and rats were crawling out of each hole. I'd never seen rats this big in my life. I watched him kick them one at a time away from him as they jumped out of the holes faster and faster. He kicked one just as another bit into his ankle. He kicked it away and fell in the process. I stood there watching as they tore into his flesh. "Where the fuck she get all of these rats?" I asked myself, as I backed away from the pit.

"That was easy. They thought I couldn't help!" I said out loud to myself. I turned around and headed towards the stairs, so I could make it home before they got back. If I leave now, even if they beat me back, I can say I just went to the store. When I got to the stairs, they shifted. I tried to step on the first step but the staircase started to slide into the wall and the cellar door slammed shut. Fear gripped my soul as I stumbled backwards and fell. I could hear faint squeaking noises and when I turned my phone around to look, I noticed the rats had filled the pit and were now using each other to climb out.

## Vanessa

I pulled up to the house and strangely, there was no black van parked out front. I climbed out of the car wondering why Aurel hadn't showed up with my payment. By the time I got to the door, Chris and Phat pulled into the yard and that's when I realized Alexis' truck was gone. Panic and fear ripped through my body as I high tailed it through the house looking for Alexis. This felt like déjà vu! I ran back into the living room, just as Phat and Chris walked in the house.

"The hell wrong with you now?" Chris asked.

"Alexis is gone," I said, as I ran to the box but it was empty. I turned around with tears streaming down my face and looked at Phat. "You let her do a hit?" I asked with a lump in my throat. I didn't give him time to answer as I ran back into their room to find the picture and tape recorder.

The picture was gone but she left the recorder, so I grabbed it and ran back into the living room. We listened to it but it didn't help us at all without having the picture because the address is on it. "Fuck!" I screamed, as I threw the tape recorder against the wall and watched it shatter into pieces and land on the floor. A loud wail came out of my body as I dropped down to the floor. She's my best friend, the only person that understands me and accepts me, and now she's gone because of me. The tape clearly says that after the job is complete, Aurel will show up with money and an address but he hasn't even showed up to pay us for the ones we just did. The last hit was a setup and since we all completed those hits at the same time, he didn't come at all.

"Where you going?" Phat asked because I stood to my feet and walked away.

"I need a minute," I tossed over my shoulder, as I headed into my room. As soon as I opened the door, I saw paper on my bed that I didn't leave there, two remotes on my nightstand, and one on my dresser. The one on my dresser was closer, so I picked it up but it lost signal. I grabbed my bag and slid it inside of it. I walked over to my nightstand and noticed one of them was labeled with an A and the other with a B, but they were both in the same place. I threw B in my bag and made my way to my bed to read the letter.

*Hey V,*

*So look don't be mad at me but I went and bought three tracking devices. I don't know why I bought three when I only needed two but something told me to get it so I did. If you're reading this then I got caught and if you guys can't save me don't blame yourself. I take full responsibility and I love you all. Anywho, tracking device A is in my pocket and B is taped under one of those Black Vans that I'm following back to Boss Lady's house.*

*Frankie*
*p.s. come save me*

As soon as I read the first sentence, all of my tears dried up. It's time out for the crybaby shit simply because my sisters are missing, and these tears ain't gone find them. I checked my bag to make sure all of my knives and grenades were in place. I slid out of my cute clothes and threw on an all-black jogging suit and Ashiko boots. I grabbed my bag and headed out to the living room. "Damn Rambo!" Chris said, failing miserably at making light of the situation.

"Let's go," I said after I made sure the remote still had the tracking devices signal.

"Where we headed?" Phat asked after we loaded up and pulled off. I told them what Frankie said in her letter.

"Maybe Lexi got the other one," Chris said.

"I hope so since Frankie didn't take it but the remote doesn't have a signal on it," I said, as I continued to drive to our destination. I was driving like a bat out of hell and it only took thirty minutes before I passed the bumpy road that I was supposed to turn on. I drove up a few more feet and hit a U-turn and turned on the road.

I drove down the bumpy road and slowed down when I saw headlights. "That's Frankie's car," I said as I threw my car in park and hopped out. Chris and Phat followed suit as I looked around the inside for any type of struggle but there wasn't one. We hopped back in the car and continued to drive until we came to a gate. I could see guard towers but I didn't see any guards. Chris got out of the car and walked up to the gate and pushed it slightly because it was ajar. It rocked but didn't open completely. "C'mon!" I yelled out of the window.

When he hopped in the car, I backed up to get a good distance before I rammed the gates and drove the rest of the way to the house. We all hopped out and made our way into the house. I pushed the door open and the sight before me made my mouth drop. It was empty. There wasn't a piece of furniture in sight. I checked the remote and I hadn't reached the tracking device, so maybe Frankie is still here.

"Aye, let's check down there," I said when I noticed the elevator. My gut was telling me not to go but I had to be sure she wasn't down there. We loaded onto the elevator that only went down and I could hear the tracking device ticking. "I didn't know these things tick when you get closer to them," I said as I followed the noise. "What the fuck?" I said, when I saw a chair facing the opposite direction with a note on top of Frankie's jacket.

*You did all of that to kill me but I ended up killing you*

"That's all it says," I shrugged after reading the note out loud. I looked at Chris and Phat and they looked as clueless as I felt. I grabbed Frankie's jacket and my heart got caught in my throat. I took a cautious step back as I peered at the bomb tied down to the chair in front of me that timed us perfectly. 10, 9, 8, 7, 6.......


## Sneak Peek to Addicted to him Part III

**Tamia**

It's been weird going to visit Rashard every day. It's been almost three weeks since he slipped into a coma and he hasn't woken up yet. I met his sister, Myra, through Candy and she had been going to the school picking up his assignments. Luckily, he took finals before this happened. Anyway, Myra gives his assignments to me and once I complete them, I turn them in. Our graduation is literally right around the corner and I'm afraid he won't be able to walk across the stage. I go sit with him at Doc's house every chance I get. I only stayed off from work a week before I returned with lifting restrictions. I was still able to get vitals on patients; I just wasn't able to assist them.

In between work and Brandon, yes I said Brandon, it's not much time left for Rashard. I like Rashard but we hadn't put any titles on anything before this happened and I was more than likely going to pull away anyway. Brandon has been my savior! I sat down at Candy's house with her and told her how I felt. It was like every time I needed to be saved, Brandon was the one to save me. It shouldn't have been Brandon; it should have been Rashard. That's why when he asked me to go out on a date with him, I agreed.

We've been kicking it really hard these past two weeks and I'm really loving the type of guy that he is. He's extremely courteous. He opens doors and pulls out chairs. He calls me daily to tell me good morning and to see how my day went, and I love the attention. We have been out on ten dates in two weeks. We haven't had sex and I'm honestly passed ready to get this box beat up. It's been years! Nobody has been in this since Amere.

I'm well aware that I can sleep with anyone I want but that's not the kind of person I am. I have a lot going for myself and I don't want to get hurt.

For me, sex is an emotional connection. I can't have sex with someone I'm not emotionally attached to. I'll never understand how Armani can just give it to any and every man that will pay for it. Well, she's not that loose but she's been screwing at least four people at once. She kept them in rotation, making sure she was always available to them all. That's a job within itself. I haven't seen her at all since she's been free from Steve and that's fine with me. I'm just glad she's ok.

"Have you started inviting people yet?" Candy asked me, snapping me out of my thoughts. I had been staying with her and everything was perfect. We get along perfectly like siblings, which in all honesty, really isn't perfect.

"I don't have anyone to invite," I stated. I looked up at her as her smile faded away. "Girl, if you don't smile, I'm going to kick yo yellow ass! I didn't do this for anyone else. This graduation is for me. It's ok," I said, giving her a reassuring smile.

"What about Armani?" she asked with a serious expression on her face. We hadn't talked about her at all after I gave her the rundown of our friendship and ended with how I found out she had been sleeping with Amere.

Speaking of Amere, he made it through and as soon as his wounds heal, he'll go through physical therapy. As far as his daughter, who wasn't really his daughter, she didn't make it. I wanted to reach out to Lisa and give her my condolences but I didn't want her to think I was trying to be funny, so I left well enough alone. A simple prayer request that God gives her strength to deal with this was all I needed to do.

"I have no idea how to get in touch with Armani," I said, looking at the TV. I heard Candy suck her teeth before walking out of the living room. I always think it's funny how Candy sucks her teeth and walks away when she has an attitude. Normally, she would say whatever she wanted to say then walk off before you can respond. What she didn't know was that when she does that to me, I will follow her to the ends of the earth to get the last word. Ding! My text message tone going off caught my attention.

**Brandon: wyd baby**

**Tamia: well, I was talkin to Candy but she walked off lol**

**Brandon: get dressed im comin to get u**

**Tamia: is that question???**

**Brandon: Did you see a question mark?**

**Tamia: ugh I wasn't planning on doing nothing today**

**Brandon: i didnt ask wat ur plans were. c u n 15**

I didn't bother responding because he's going to come anyway. When we first started talking, his aggressive attitude was a major turn on. Sometimes it still is but when I don't really want to be bothered and he does it, it's aggravating. Candy warned me about him and I didn't listen. She told me it was only going to get worse but it hasn't. I always make sure I tell him we're just friends, so it's not like I'm leading him on or anything. For some reason, I'm holding on to the little hope I have that Rashard will get better and we will be together. That's just wishful thinking though.

I like Brandon but there's just something eerie about him. He has this gloomy presence about him when we aren't talking. It's hard to describe but I'll try. Have you ever been around someone and whether you're, talking, laughing or being quiet, it's peaceful? Well, with Brandon, as long as we're laughing or talking, it's fine. When we aren't talking, the silence is deadly. That's why

I'm never alone with him unless we're in the car. We have been on plenty of dates but it's never a chill at his place type of thing.

"Hey Candy!" I yelled walking to her room. When I got to the door, she signaled for me to give her a moment with her finger. I could see the smile on her face and she was shaking her leg.

"Ok, we will be right over," she said before she hung the phone up. She turned to face me with a smile on her face. "Bitch, what the hell you smiling for?" she asked me. I didn't realize I was smiling until she said that.

"I don't know. Why we happy?" I asked laughing.

"Because Rashard is awake!" she said jumping up and down. My jaw hit the floor.

"Where you goin?" Candy yelled at my back because I ran out of her room.

"I have to get dressed so we can go!" I yelled over my shoulder. I rummaged through my clothes until I found some dark blue jean skinny legs. I rolled the bottom of them up to my calf to bring attention to the brown sandals that I wore wrapped around my ankles. I threw on a bright yellow cropped top shirt that read "I'm Yours" across my small breasts. I grabbed a brown belt to match the shoes and I was good to go. I hadn't had my hair done since Deuce's birthday party, so I just threw it up in a messy bun and let a few curly strands dangle around my face.

"Ok, I'm ready," I said, walking in the living room to an already dressed Candy. She wore a long flowing multicolored maxi dress. Her thong style sandals were also multicolored. She wore silver accessories with her hair in a tight ponytail.

"You said that like it took you five minutes when I've been sitting in here for ten," she said, as she rolled her eyes playfully at me.

"Oh hush, let's go!" I exclaimed as walked swiftly to the front door.

I swung the door open and ran directly into Brandon. I was so excited about Rashard being awake that I wasn't paying any attention to where I was going. When I bumped into him, he dropped his phone, which is probably why we ran into each other. "I'm sorry," I said, reaching down to pick the pieces to his phone up. He grabbed me and pulled me out of reach of his phone and picked it up himself. A frown graced his handsome face.

"You good," he said, as he put the pieces back together.
Candy walked out of the house reminding me that Rashard is awake. I stood there looking between Candy and Brandon. She had a smirk on her face and he hadn't looked up yet. "Hey Brandon, I can't go with you," I said nervously. I have no idea why I'm nervous but I am. In the two weeks, I've never had to tell him no and stick with it. He's always been able to get me to change my mind or rearrange my plans. The only thing he never tried to interfere with was work and that's because I let him know upfront that it was very important to me. Trying to stop me from getting the hours could mess with me graduating on time and as far as I've come, I was not about to let a man come between me and success.

"The fuck you mean you can't come?" he asked, then looked over at Candy.

"Hey, don't look at me," she said with her hands up. "I'll be in my truck," she said to me as she walked passed me to get her truck.

"Rashard is awake. We're going to see him," I explained, as I fiddled with my fingernails.

"Oh ok. Well, call me later," he said and walked away. I was shocked that it went so well but glad it did.

## Candy

Living with Tamia has been peachy but I really wish she had listened to me and not got involved with Brandon. Sure, he's handsome and charming and don't get me started on his eyes, but that's like the calm before the storm. I'm a friend to them both so I couldn't exactly indulge too much, but I let her know he's crazy and suggested that she not talk to him. I've known Brandon awhile and Deuce has known him even longer, being as though they're family and even he asked me why I hook that up. Truth be told, their little match up had nothing to do with me. I'm so glad Rashard is ready to get up because I need him to step up for Tamia and take her away from Brandon.

When I got the call to come to Doc's house, I was overjoyed with emotions because I've been witnessing the stress him being out of pocket has caused Tamia. I really think she's been through enough already but now she's starting to make dumb choices. Most girls get mad when they find out later on down the line that the nigga they fucking with is crazy, but I told her as soon as I saw she was interested. I noticed she fought the attraction for a good week after the accident but I wish she would have held out a little longer. I tried telling Rashard to get it together but being a friend to Tamia, I couldn't tell him why. Rashard has been having this ongoing issue that he's been trying to fix, but I'm going to let him tell you about that.

When I walked out of the house behind Tamia and saw Brandon, I shook my head. Nigga had the nerve to look at me like I'm the reason she's cancelling a probably, unplanned, date. I just went ahead to my truck and called Deuce.

"What's up?" he answered. I could barely hear him over the music but he's always in a noisy environment.

"Can you turn that down for a minute?" I asked with my face screwed up. We finally made this thing official but now we're taking things one day at a time because neither one of us are used to being in a relationship.

"Lemme walk outta here," he said. I crunk my truck up as I waited for him to leave out of the noisy room he was in. "What you got going?" he asked, once he was outside.

"Rashard is ready," I said.

"Finally? Took his ass long enough," he said with this nonchalant attitude. Deuce is the only one, other than myself, that Rashard trusts and I think it's because Rashard knows I trust Deuce.

"Tell me about it," I said, as I watched Tamia and Brandon have a quick exchange.
"Look, I gotta go but I need you to keep a handle on Brandon for me; you know how he gets," I said quickly.

"Man that man grown as fuck," Deuce said.

"Yea but he's crazy too and this my girl," I said.

"And I'm yo nigga and he my cousin! Leave that shit between them. Shit, you did yo part, now mind yo business. Call me later," he said and hung the phone up in my ear. I pulled the phone away from my ear and stared at the phone in disbelief. I let out a deep frustrated breath as I watched Tamia walk to the truck.

"That was easy," she said, as she snapped her seatbelt on.

"Too easy," I replied, as I looked behind me. Brandon was taking his time getting in his all black Charger and letting me out. Shit, we couldn't go anywhere until he moved from behind us but it looked like he was playing on his phone. "What the fuck?" I asked and gestured for Tamia to look back. When she looked at what I was looking at, she rolled her eyes and sat back against the seat.

I laid on the horn to get his attention. It must have pissed him off because he backed his car up and burned rubber. I peeled off in the opposite direction. *I hope like hell Rashard knows what he's doing*, I thought to myself as I shook my head.

"What's wrong Candy?" Tamia asked. I glanced over at her as she rotated her body, so she could face me. I couldn't tell her what I was I thinking. "It sucks being caught in the middle," is what I wanted to say.

"Deuce's childish ass," is what I actually said.

"What he do?" she asked, but I just shook my head and turned the music up.

Funny thing is, the song that started playing is perfect for Rashard's current predicament. I bobbed my head to smooth blues song by Carl Mims as he sang about being caught up in a two-way love affair. I glanced over at Tamia and she had tears in her eyes. I thought about the lyrics of the song and as fucked up as it is, it's perfect for her too.

Being that I'm friends with them all, it's not much I can do at this moment but change the station. The song made with Drake and Wayne called *Only* blared through the speakers. "I never fucked Wayne. I never fucked Drake," Nicki Minaj said, which wasn't any better since Tamia hadn't fucked Rashard or Brandon.

*Fuck it, this my song. Tamia gonna have to tough it out*, I thought myself as I continued to drive. I glanced over at her and she still had tears welled up in her eyes but she didn't let them fall. I'm not going to push the issue because I honestly just don't feel like I can hold anymore secrets. Hell, lately I've been wanting to just quit talking to all these mufuckers because they're all forcing me to keep secrets that I didn't ask to hold.

A few minutes later, I was pulling up to Doc's house. I took a deep breath and looked over at Tamia. She was so excited that she didn't wait for me to get out before she was walking to the door. "God, please don't let this go left," I said out loud. I shook my head and followed her to the door.

**Rashard**

I sat in Doc's living room a nervous fucking wreck after I told Candy that I was finally ready to face the music. Chardae is indeed pregnant and she's far enough along to know what she's having. It's a boy. Wait, let me take you back so you won't be confused.

The day of the accident, I passed out on my way to Doc's house. Well, we were in the operating room alone when I woke up. I gave Doc a quick rundown on the bullshit that was happening in my life and he agreed to help me out. I gave him $6,000 to make Tamia think I was in a coma while I got things straightened out with Chardae. Call it what you want but I'm not trying to lose Tamia.

Anyway, Doc has it set up to where she has to call before she comes. After she calls him, he calls me, and I leave Chardae and come back to Doc's house where he puts me under until Tamia leaves. Now Candy knows what's been going on and believe me, she curses me out every damn chance she gets, but I know Candy will never betray me.

Before you go to turning your nose up at me for making Tamia think I've been in a coma, try thinking about it from my side of things. I've just really started to get close to Tamia and I know the possibility of me having a child will ruin that. Tamia deserves a life that only I can provide for her. All I want to do is make her fall in love with me before Chardae has the baby. That way, if the baby is mine, she won't want to leave me and if it isn't then we won't have a problem at all. Either way, I'm not telling her about Chardae possibly being pregnant with my child. Hell, she's not going to know a thing about a baby until after the results, and that's only if the baby is mine.

"I think you should wait in the bed she's been visiting you in," Doc suggested.

"Why?" I asked with a confused look on my face.

"A person that's been in a coma for three weeks doesn't just get up and walk away, Shard. Tamia is smart as fuck and she will know something is off," Doc explained.

"Iight," I said, as I stood to my feet. I got up to follow him to the back just as his front door was opening. "Fuck!" I said softly to myself.

**ADDICTED TO HIM III COMING SOON....**

TRUE GLORY PUBLICATIONS

IF YOU WOULD LIKE TO BE A PART OF OUR TEAM, PLEASE SEND YOUR SUBMISSIONS BY EMAIL TO TRUEGLORYPUBLICATIONS@GMAIL.COM. PLEASE INCLUDE A BRIEF BIO, A SYNOPSIS OF THE BOOK, AND THE FIRST THREE CHAPTERS. SUBMIT USING MICROSOFT WORD WITH FONT IN 11 TIMES NEW ROMAN.

Check Out These Other Great Books By This Author

A Crazy Ghetto Love Story

Addicted To Him

Addicted To Him II

Check Out These Other Great Books From True Glory
Publishing

What You Took From Me 3: Loving An Opportunist

The Pleasure Of Pain